For Andrea,
Thank You for your support
Best wishes,
x, Jen

DEUCE

JEN SILVER

ALSO BY JEN SILVER

Single Stories:

Calling Home
Changing Perspectives
Running From Love
Christmas at Winterbourne
The Circle Dance

Starling Hill Trilogy:

Starting Over
Arc Over Time
Carved in Stone

Short Stories:

There Was a Time
The Christmas Sweepstake (Affinity's 2014 Christmas Collection)
Beltane in Space (It's in Her Kiss—Affinity Charity Anthology)
Maybe This Christmas (Affinity's Christmas Medley 2017)

DEUCE

JEN SILVER

Affinity
Rainbow Publications

2019

Deuce
© 2019 by Jen Silver

Affinity E-Book Press NZ LTD
Canterbury, New Zealand

1st Edition

ISBN: 978-1-98-854997-2

All rights reserved.

No part of this book may be reproduced in any form without the express permission of the author and publisher. Please note that piracy of copyrighted materials violate the author's rights and is Illegal.

This is a work of fiction. Names, character, places, and incidents are the product of the author's imagination or are used fictitiously and any resemblance to actual persons living or dead, businesses, companies, events, or locales is entirely coincidental

Editor: JoSelle Vanderhooft
Proof Editor: Alexis Smith
Cover Design: Irish Dragon Design
Production Design: Affinity Publication Services

Acknowledgments

During the writing of this book I revisited the selkie legends of the Scottish islands and, further north, the Faroe Islands.

In these stories, handed down to each generation, the seal people, selkies as they're called in Scotland, come ashore and shed their skins to take on human forms. They are reputed to be beautiful, handsome beings, gentle souls – but beguiling to ordinary mortals. Attempts to keep them from returning to the sea by stealing and hiding their seal skins generally leads to disaster and heartbreak.

The cover image is of the statue of Kópakonan—the seal woman—who features in a well-known folktale in the Faroe Islands.

I would like to thank Affinity for taking the chance on publishing what may seem like a fairly improbable premise for a romance.

DEDICATION

For Anne, with love, always

Table of Contents

Prologue	1
PART ONE	4
Chapter One	5
Chapter Two	16
Chapter Three	29
Chapter Four	52
Chapter Five	66
Chapter Six	78
Chapter Seven	89
PART TWO	101
Chapter Eight	102
Chapter Nine	109
Chapter Ten	115
PART THREE	123
Chapter Eleven	124
Chapter Twelve	136
Chapter Thirteen	149
Chapter Fourteen	160
Chapter Fifteen	169
Chapter Sixteen	181
PART FOUR	191
Chapter Seventeen	192
Chapter Eighteen	199
Chapter Nineteen	206
Epilogue	223
About the Author	227
Other Affinity Books	228

Deuce

PROLOGUE

I recall that the day started as many other days had for Katrin Nielsen, and I watch it now like a movie reel unfurling in my mind...

Once she had seen Konrad off to his morning lessons, Katrin washed their breakfast dishes and tied her hair back to stop it blowing across her face on the short walk to the library, such as it was; a grand name for the single-room turf-roofed hut. She was looking forward to opening the new shipment of books that had arrived from Copenhagen the day before. The books would need to be covered and catalogued but that was a job she enjoyed.

She sniffed the air when she left her work to go home at lunchtime. Only ten of the new books had been processed. Katrin always stretched the job out to make the most of the brief respite from the regular daily chore of gutting fish from the night trawlers' catches.

Konrad came racing up the path towards her before she reached their house. She loved the way he moved. Fourteen years old and all long limbs and awkwardness. He reminded her of someone she'd once known. A flicker of recognition that came and went like a lighthouse beam piercing the night.

"Mamma. Come. There's a seal on the sand. It's stranded."

Katrin gathered her coat closer to her body and followed her son down the winding path to the small strip of beach that was only visible at low tide. A few of her neighbours were already there standing around the large mammal lying on its side.

"Is it ill?" she heard one of them ask.

Katrin moved closer until she could see the creature clearly. "No. It's not ill. Seals do this from time to time. Haul out so they can rest, digest a big meal. She will rejoin the sea on the next incoming tide."

Konrad was staring at her open-mouthed, as was her nearest neighbour, Lars. She looked past them, past the recumbent seal, to the waves beginning the cycle of return to the shore. Her mind left them there, reverberations in her head, the swell of the sea, frantic shouts, holding on and holding on, wet, cold, pulling and pushing, falling into darkness....

"Mamma!" A boy's anxious face came into focus.

"What?"

"Are you okay? You said something now in a foreign language. About the seal."

"It will be okay. It's resting."

Deuce

As I turned away and walked back up the steep path, so many images rushed through my thoughts—faces, and one in particular. A name. Jay. Where was she? I had to get back to Jay and my baby. A small bundle in my arms, tiny fist curling and uncurling…and one thought gained prominence as I reached the cliff top…I am Charlotte Summersbridge.

Jen Silver

PART ONE

Deuce

CHAPTER ONE

The lane leading up to the house was little more than a farm track, deep ruts on either side of the strip of grass. Tess checked her satnav. The image on the screen clearly showed a turn into the unnamed lane. Her destination lay at the end of it, only thirty seconds away. She thought she'd heard the name of the cottage as Sea View, but the small wooden sign pointing up the lane read "Seal View." Hoping the undercarriage of her car wouldn't suffer, she maneuvered it slowly round the corner. No horrible scraping noises alerted her to possible damage.

When the reclusive Jay Reid agreed to see her, Tess had envisioned meeting in a London hotel. However, the retired tennis player's business manager, Mo Farrell, made it clear Jay spent most weekends away from the city, and the winter months always found her sequestered on the lonely stretch of coastline near Hunstanton from Friday to Monday.

Had she taken up bird watching? Tess couldn't think of much else to occupy anyone out here on the eastern edge of England. An edge that was receding further away from the continent each year as if the shoreline had a Brexit plan of its own.

Birds of the non-feathered variety were mainly what she hoped to ferret out on this visit. Jay Reid's reputation for bedding young players on the tour had outweighed her achievements of winning two Grand Slam titles and briefly holding the number-one spot in the world rankings.

Getting her to name names wouldn't be easy. No one had come forward in the twenty-three years since Jay's retirement from the tour. The adage of "what happens on tour stays on tour" seemed to have held true. But with the revelations of, mainly male, abuse of power hitting the headlines every day, Tess wondered how long it would be before someone would indulge in a "kiss and tell" story from Jay's past.

She had seen the photos, watched the videos. Jay Reid's meteoric tennis career shone brightly for eight years, then crashed and burned. At twenty-seven years old, the British star seemed to have no barriers to continuing to play at a high level for many years to come.

With the expanse of North Sea shining in the distance, the cottage came into view when she rounded the last bend. The squat grey building looked like an extension of the landscape. Visiting on a sunny day made it less bleak, but Tess could imagine how desolate it would look on a windswept rainy day, which was likely most of the year on this coastline. She parked behind a battered-looking Land Rover—one of the old models, the green paintwork daubed with mud, giving it the look of an abandoned army vehicle.

Deuce

The gleaming chrome of the motorbike next to it looked more like the kind of transport Jay would use.

Tess grabbed her bag from the front seat and climbed out of her two-year-old Honda Civic. She did a quick inventory to make sure she had her camera, recorder, and notebook. Unnecessary, as she'd checked three times before leaving home early that morning. Walking past the Land Rover and the bike, she was greeted with an unexpected view of a well-tended garden, sloping down from a patio.

A woman came out of the open doors and stood looking at the view before turning to acknowledge Tess.

She hoped the shock didn't show on her face. The photos she'd studied showed a tall, athletic figure with androgynous good looks. Jay Reid was only fifty years old. Surely she hadn't shrunk so much or acquired so many lines on her face. Perhaps she had a drink or drugs problem.

The woman came closer. "Hi, we spoke on the phone. I'm Mo."

"Oh. Of course." Tess hoped her smile covered her initial reaction. She held out her hand, "Pleased to meet you."

"Jay will be out in a few minutes." Mo shook her hand with a strong grip. "I'll leave you to it. You've got my number." Nothing resembling a smile crossed her features, and she brushed past Tess after letting go of her hand.

The roar of the motorbike shattered another of her misjudgments since her arrival. She shook her head.

†

A flock of seagulls wheeled away from her line of sight. Whatever had attracted them to the shore below had no doubt been hoovered up in their greedy beaks. Jay glanced at the timer. Another ten minutes. She kept her legs moving.

Spinning. An apt metaphor for her life, wheels turning, going nowhere.

The journalist would be here in half an hour. As soon as Jay had finally given Mo the go-ahead to tell the woman she would talk to her, Jay had had second thoughts. Did she really want to rake up the past? She had always been thankful her career ended before the advent of social media. A few paparazzi could be shaken off, but not now when seemingly everyone carried a mobile device capable of taking pictures and sending them out to the world. Her secrets would have been public knowledge in no time.

Fifty years old, half her life gone if she lived to a hundred. Half her life wasted. Why would anyone want to read about that? She started the five-minute cool-down and reminded herself she was doing it for Charley and the seals. Nothing else mattered. Her successes on the tennis courts, her conquests in bed, those were the moments the journalist would want her to talk about. But that wasn't Jay's over-riding passion any longer. It hadn't been since she quit the circuit. The only thing that mattered, the one thing she had never publicly spoken of…the loss of the love of her life. Could she ever manage to explain what the world…her world…had lost when Charley and the rest of the research team disappeared into the depths of the North Sea?

Losing tennis matches had threatened at times to overwhelm her emotionally. But there was always another day, another game, and another chance to win. Losing Charley hit her harder than anything else she'd faced up to that point in her life. By the age of sixteen, she had already lost her parents to a car crash, and then four years later, her older brother to an oil-platform explosion only days after she won her first Grand Slam match. It was no wonder she held on tightly to what had been left to her—the baby she and Charley had planned to bring up together.

Mo called out from the kitchen, "I'm leaving now. The coffee pot's set up. You just need to switch it on."

"Thanks." Jay stepped off the exercise bike and walked around the screen as Mo entered the conservatory. "I have time for a quick shower, don't I?"

"Definitely. And don't come any closer. You smell pretty ripe even from here."

Jay flicked the towel at her. "Go, then. I'll see you on Monday."

"And play nice!" was Mo's parting shot as she left.

"Don't I always?" Jay muttered, heading for the shower.

†

"I never get tired of the view."

Tess turned to face the speaker. Jay Reid in person. She could have stepped straight off a tennis court, dressed in shorts and a form-fitting T-shirt. If Tess hadn't known her age, she would have thought Jay was closer to forty than fifty.

A small dog trotted out from behind Jay's legs. Tess held out a hand for it to sniff. She wasn't a dog person, but she knew this was a safe way to let the animal approach.

"He doesn't bite."

After a cursory sniff, the dog licked her fingers, then settled down under the wooden bench next to the conservatory door.

"He's cute. What breed is he?'

"Boston terrier. Coffee?"

"Yes, thanks. Would you mind if I used your loo first?"

"No, of course not. On your right, past the kitchen."

Tess's first impressions proved wrong again. The conservatory, kitchen, and bathroom were all outfitted like an IKEA showroom. A quick peek into the sitting room revealed the aspect she'd expected: dark, authentic wooden beams not far above her head, and a stone fireplace at one end. For a moment, a strange feeling assaulted her. A sense she'd been here before. She'd never really believed in it, but it was a clear déjà-vu moment. Tess shook her head. She had never been to this part of the country in her life.

Jay had set out the coffee mugs on a table in the conservatory. Tess sat in the cushioned chair her host indicated. She hoped she was getting this first impression wrong as well. So far, the subject of her visit didn't seem too thrilled to see her. None of the usual introductory pleasantries, asking about her journey, or even introducing herself. Obviously Tess knew who Jay was, and Jay knew she was coming. Still, it made her feel uncomfortable, off balance. Maybe that was the intention.

She helped herself to milk and a spoonful of sugar. The clatter of her spoon against the side of the mug brought the terrier back inside. He looked at the plate of digestive biscuits on the table, then up at Jay.

"No, Ritchie. They're not for you."

He seemed to understand and sat by Jay's feet. She fondled his ears before reaching for her own mug. No milk or sugar for her. No wonder she looked trim for her age.

Tess had interviewed many people, some who were more willing to talk than others. She always got through in the end. But something about Jay Reid made her think this was going to be a particularly difficult task.

"When you've finished your drink, we'll go down to the beach."

Deuce

"Okay." She looked at her shoes. They were comfortable for walking, but she wished she wasn't wearing a skirt. An October breeze off the North Sea wasn't what she'd bargained for. But if walking would get Jay talking, then she would have to go with it.

†

The poor girl looked frozen by the time they walked back from the beach. So Jay led the way into the sitting room and got the fire started. It would take a few minutes for the flames to catch and start consuming the logs. Ritchie claimed his place by the hearth.

"Tea or coffee?" Jay would have offered something stronger, but Tess had a long drive ahead of her.

"Tea would be lovely, thanks."

When Jay returned with the tray, Tess had set up her laptop. She moved it to one side of the low table to make room. With the tea poured and fire starting to crackle, Jay gave in to the inevitable purpose of the journalist's visit.

Tess asked the usual questions about her early years. Talking about her parents didn't get any easier with the passing of time. And she didn't want to talk about Stewart. After deflecting those prompts, she moved on to the start of her tennis career. How she was self-taught, with her brother finally convinced it was the best way forward for her, after only two terms at university. They'd both learned the hard way that life was short. Her goal had been to play at Wimbledon, and she couldn't believe her luck when she got a wild card into the tournament after only her first year on the tour. Two semi-final finishes had brought her to the attention of the higher echelons of the tennis world.

"You've seen the tapes, I guess."

Tess nodded eagerly.

Jay didn't need a visual reminder of that day. Her first win...and on the fabled grass of Wimbledon's Centre Court. The only thing she expected to take away from the tournament was a coveted green-and-purple branded towel. Since she was a wild-card entrant the crowd didn't expect much from her either. Until she reached the fourth round...then the semi final, and the final. Virginia Wade's 1977 win was a faint memory in the minds of even the most ardent British tennis fans.

Jay won the toss and let her opponent serve. Why? A question that was asked many times during the first set. Games went with serve for the first five, then she was broken and lost the first set 6–2.

Her opponent won the first game off her in the second set. Jay returned to her seat aware that the crowd was with her all the way now. She was sure to lose, but she was all theirs, British through and through. It was inconceivable that she could win. She looked up from behind her towel and smiled. The cameras picked up that smile, and commentators remarked how relaxed she looked considering the tremendous pressure she was under.

Jay led the way out for the next set, and the crowd had to be told to be quiet as her opponent prepared to serve. From then on, Jay outplayed her, frustrated her at every hard-won point until serious errors took their toll. So it finished with scores in her favour at 2–6, 6–1, 6–0. The spectators couldn't believe it. They had watched her demolish the highest-ranked player in the tournament with seeming ease in the last two sets.

Deuce

When she saw the video of the match a few days later, the cringe-making remarks of the commentators were embarrassing. They sounded almost upset, apologetic even, that she'd won.

Tess looked up from her laptop. "There was a pitch invasion when you won, wasn't there?"

"I suppose you could call it that. Totally flummoxed the officials. They were gearing up for the usual sedate ceremony. I certainly didn't expect to be carried around the court by a group of well-dressed toffs chanting, 'We are the champions'. The Duchess of Kent, of course, didn't let it fluster her."

"What did she say to you?"

"I really don't remember. 'Well played', or something to that effect."

The girl's next comments shouldn't have come as a surprise. She had obviously researched Jay's career thoroughly before coming to see her.

"Your brother and his girlfriend were in the players' box. That must have meant a lot to you."

"His girlfriend? Oh, you mean Charley." Jay struggled to keep her emotions in check. "Yes, it meant a lot that they were there that day." She stood and walked over to the window. "Looks like a storm front's moving in. You might want to leave now to get back onto the main road before it hits."

†

Tess drove away, more questions than answers seething through her thoughts. The alleged storm didn't materialise until she had reached Norwich and parked in the pub car park. As she suspected, Jay had used the weather as an excuse to get rid of her. When she reached her room, Tess texted Alice to let her know she was staying overnight and could FaceTime with her when she got home from work.

The Wi-Fi was good enough to let her do some Internet searching, and the first name she typed in was *Stewart Reid*. She already knew his was one of the bodies not recovered after the Piper Alpha platform explosion. Just three days after seeing his sister win the Women's Wimbledon final. Further searches led to a brief bio of the petroleum engineer and the fact his only surviving relative was a Julie Ann Reid.

Tess could have kicked herself for not picking up on this before. When she'd googled Jay Reid initially, the information connected to that name and the Wikipedia entry only mentioned her tennis career.

Julie Ann Reid was also a common name so she got a lot of hits, but Tess found her easily enough now, listed as the managing director and senior consultant at CSC, a physical therapy clinic in London which helped injured athletes and armed-forces personnel get back on their feet, sometimes quite literally. J. A. Reid, BSc, MCSP, CSP, HSPC...an impressive list attesting to her professional qualifications. The full name of the business only appeared on the *about us* page on the website, causing another mental jolt for Tess. CSC stood for Charlotte Summersbridge Clinic.

Falling back onto the bed, Tess closed her eyes. It was almost too much to take in. When she had first seen the footage of that Wimbledon final, the camera had focused often on Stewart Reid and his companion between serves. Large sunglasses and a wide-brimmed straw hat obscured most of the woman's face but something about her struck a chord. Now she knew why. Jay had called her Charley, but Tess had known her as Auntie Char.

†

Jay paced up and down, kicking at a loose stone on the patio. Tess Bailey-Roberts. No reason she should have recognised the name. But the face was all too familiar. She couldn't blame Mo. Her friend and agent hadn't known Charley or Stewart and she hadn't met the girl, only arranged the meeting on the phone.

Taking her for a walk along the beach had helped assuage the tightness in her chest. Jay had succeeded in giving out little personal information apart from her involvement as a volunteer in the mammal-watch programme. But back in the cottage, answering questions and reliving her first Grand Slam win, she'd had to find an excuse to end the conversation.

The girl was no fool. She would have realised soon enough that Jay had wanted to get rid of her. Although Jay had agreed to meet up again in London the following week, she would ask Mo to cancel.

Chapter Two

"What did you tell her?" Mo gave the salad a final toss and brought the bowl to the table.

Jay handed her a glass of red wine and sat. "Not a lot. She asked about my tennis career. That's all anyone wants to know about me. It's all they need to know."

"Not quite all."

"Of course she wants to know what I've done since then. So I took her down to the beach."

Mo smothered a laugh. "Poor girl. She wasn't dressed for a hike."

"Hey, she'd driven all that way. Might as well have a close-up look at the sea. I think she enjoyed it."

"A lecture on marine conservation wouldn't have been high on her list of topics."

Jay pushed the lettuce to the edge of her plate. "Well, she must be a good actor. Either that or she has a high threshold for boredom. Didn't yawn once."

"Did you make another appointment to see her again?"

"I did."

Mo wished she had been able to convince Jay to see a therapist all those years ago. She hoped the journalist could draw Jay out. Her employer's next words shut that idea down.

"But I want you to cancel." Jay finished her wine and poured another generous measure.

Mo saw the darkness lurking in her friend's eyes, something that usually only showed up on three significant dates throughout the year. "Why? Did she upset you in some way?" Mo didn't think the attractive young woman she'd met outside the cottage looked at all threatening. "Oh shit. You made a pass at her."

"Fuck no!" Jay gulped some more wine.

"What, then?" Mo moved the wine glass away. "No more of this until you tell me."

Jay sighed and leant back in her chair. "She's Charley's daughter."

"Charley had another child?" Mo reached for her own glass of wine. She thought she knew all the details of Jay's early life, but this was news.

"She was in her third year at Uni and wanted to carry on to do a Masters. But the course involved a lot of travel expenses that her scholarship fund wouldn't cover. So she agreed to be a surrogate for these two women she knew. One had been her biology teacher in high school. They were both over thirty and wanted a child but neither of them were able to carry one."

Mo pushed Jay's wine glass back across the table. "Wow. And this Tess is the result?"

"Yeah. Apart from her looks, she's the right age. And she has her father's eyes."

"You knew the sperm donor?"

Jay took another slug of wine. "My brother."

"Christ! So that means you're her aunt." Mo sipped her wine. "Biologically-speaking, that is."

"Got it in one. Charley didn't talk about her much. I knew she visited the family on occasion, usually when I was at a tournament abroad."

"Does the girl know?"

"If she does, she didn't let on."

"Are you going to let Josh know he has a sister?"

"No."

"Why not? He might like to know he has a family, apart from you."

"We've done all right."

Jay's steely look alerted Mo to the fact she had overstepped the mark, again. But sometimes Jay needed a prod. "Of course you have. If you've finished pushing that tomato around your plate I'll get the stew."

†

Jay knew she was only fooling herself if she thought Tess was easily put off. If she even had a fraction of Charley's determination she wouldn't let go until she'd ferreted out the truth.

"What have you got on this week?" Mo asked, placing the dish of irish stew on the table.

Jay didn't think she would be able to eat anything, but the aroma was enticing and she appreciated the change of subject. "Some new clients at the clinic. Seeing Amanda tonight. Taking Josh out for dinner tomorrow."

Deuce

They ate in silence until both their plates were empty. Jay shook her head when Mo offered her another helping.

"No thanks, I'm stuffed."

"What time do you need to be at Amanda's?"

"She said she'd be home by eight, but there's no rush." Jay glanced at her watch. Eight thirty-five. Even if Amanda did get back to her flat on time she'd want to shower and change.

"You're not wearing your engagement ring."

"I've told her I can't wear it when I'm working."

"You're not working now."

"Or when I'm working out or making love, so there doesn't seem much point in taking it on and off between those times."

"You're a shit fiancée."

"I know."

"The wedding is in three weeks. Have you even thought about what you're going to wear?"

"Don't fret. It's all good. I've left Friday afternoon free this week. Josh and I are going suit shopping together."

"You're not buying something off the peg. This is going to be a classy affair."

"Yeah, I thought we'd pop into Marks..." Jay laughed at the look on Mo's face. "Honestly, you'd think you were the mother of the bride. Relax. We've got an appointment with a tailor on Savile Row."

"Have you met her parents yet?"

"No. Considering she's their only child, they don't seem in any rush to meet me. Her mother's more concerned about missing a few operas in Venice. And her dad's always somewhere between Dubai and New York. I get the feeling it would be different if she were marrying a man."

"Oh. You mean because it's two women, it doesn't really count?"

"Exactly. And then there's Josh. Will they want to accept him as part of their family?"

Mo put a hand on her arm. "Hey. I'm sure that won't be an issue. Everyone loves Josh. And, believe it or not, he's a grown-up now, quite capable of fighting his own corner."

"Yeah, I just can't help worrying about him."

†

Amanda checked her watch again. The cab had only moved a few feet since the last time she looked. She would be lucky to make it back to her flat by nine at the rate they weren't moving. Walking was out of the question with the rain pelting down. She should have left the pub earlier, but joining colleagues for an after-work drink helped maintain Jay's idea of her lifestyle as a City high-flyer.

She sat back and closed her eyes. Jay had a key and could make herself at home. Maybe they could shower together. That thought and the images that followed sustained her through the next few minutes of tortuously slow progress.

It was ten past nine when she made it through the door of her penthouse flat. "Honey, I'm home," she called, removing her shoes, sodden just from the short trip from the taxi to the door of the building.

There was no answer and the living room was in darkness. Amanda adjusted the light switch to an ambient glow. Fumbling in her bag, she pulled out her phone to see if Jay had left a message. Ever since their engagement, her lover had been increasingly lax with her timekeeping. That would have to change once they were married. These mysterious weekends at some unspecified location would have to stop as well. She didn't mind Jay spending the evening with Mo, although even she seemed to have taken a vow of secrecy about these excursions. Jay had muttered something once about training. But Jay didn't need to train. She kept in shape though, and Amanda appreciated that. Josh had proven just as tight-lipped on Jay's movements on the few times she'd got the boy alone.

Still, only a few weeks to go. Once they were wife and wife, there would be no secrets between them. Amanda shed her wet clothing as she walked down the hall. She dropped the garments off in the laundry room before heading into the bathroom.

†

The shower was running when Jay entered the flat. She dropped her passkey on the small table by the door and wandered into the living room. The view along the river at night always caught her attention. She stood by the window and gazed at the lights on Tower Bridge, almost close enough to reach out and touch.

Amanda wouldn't have been able to afford this place even with her high level of earnings over the last fifteen years. Her father had snapped up some riverside real estate when the warehouses were abandoned. Prices for these flats now were in the multi-millions.

Jay never felt entirely comfortable here. Another thing they hadn't really discussed; where they would live after the wedding. She didn't want to leave her mews house in Kensington. It was now also worth millions, but when she'd bought it with what was left of her share of her parents' life insurance, it had been almost derelict. The remainder of the prize money from her tennis successes enabled her to give it a complete makeover. It had been enhanced further by Josh's architectural embellishments, which had formed part of his final-year university project.

And then there was the cottage that Amanda knew nothing about. It had been Charley's dream to live there, at least part-time. She wanted to be close to the Sea Life Sanctuary at Hunstanton so she could offer her services to the seal-rescue centre and hospital. Shortly before she disappeared, Charley had started training to be a marine-mammal medic.

Leaning her head against the glass, her breath misting up the view, Jay made the decision to put off making a decision. For the foreseeable future, Josh could continue to live at the mews with Ritchie. Escaping to the cottage at weekends would be more problematic, though. Perhaps she could tell Amanda she was in the Territorial Army and had to train regularly to be battle-ready in case of regular army shortages in Afghanistan. Unlikely she would be sent there at her age, even if she were in the TA.

Arms reached around her waist, and Amanda's heady jasmine-scented aroma enveloped her senses.

"Hey, babe. What are you thinking about?"

Jay hated being called babe. But she didn't want to start an argument. As she pushed back from the glass, Amanda had to loosen her grip or fall over. Jay turned and repositioned the naked woman's arms about her torso and bent her head for a kiss. It was easy to deflect Amanda's questions and she couldn't speak with Jay's tongue probing her mouth. The moans that did escape were an invitation to keep going.

†

Deuce

It was still dark when Amanda opened her eyes. She was an early riser, always in the office by eight thirty and ready to go. Unlike many of her colleagues who stumbled in at nine o'clock bleary-eyed, clutching mega cups of triple-shot coffees.

Memories of the night before washed over her as she breathed in the evidence of their extensive lovemaking. Just the thought of Jay's tongue giving her pleasure had her insides churning again. It took her another moment to realise she was alone in the bed. Reaching for her phone, she checked the time. Six thirty-five.

Damned if she was going to let her lover leave without giving her what she needed. Hoping to catch her in the bathroom, she was disappointed to find it empty, although the shower walls were still steamy from recent use.

Jay was in the kitchen, fully dressed and draining a glass of orange juice.

"You don't have go yet, do you?"

"Yeah. I've got to go home and change before work."

"You should start leaving some clothes here. Then you wouldn't have to leave so early." Amanda pressed herself against Jay, giving her no option other than to hold her. "I'm so ready for you. Please, Jay. I need you inside me now."

Jay's expression was hard to read; her eyes darkened with either rage or lust, Amanda didn't know. She'd trapped Jay's leg between her own and could feel her arousal soaking into her lover's jeans.

With seemingly little effort, Jay disentangled herself, and Amanda felt the loss keenly. But then Jay stroked a hand down her cheek, continuing down her body, lingering long enough to tweak a nipple. Amanda closed her eyes, anticipating the feel of those long fingers moving inside her again. She was so ready, the insides of her thighs already coated in moisture. She wriggled with pleasure as Jay's hand pressed against her mound and the questing fingers teased apart the wet curls.

Amanda cried out, each slow stroke bringing her closer to the edge. "Deeper, please, Jay!" But with only one more gentle touch pressing lightly against her engorged folds of tender skin, she lost control, crying out Jay's name over and over.

Jay removed her hand, grabbed a few pieces of paper towel, and left without a backward glance.

"Jay!" Amanda eased herself away from the counter. She reached the outer door in time to see it closing. Naked and dripping, she couldn't run after her. Legs trembling from the effects of her most recent orgasm, she collapsed onto the floor, wrapped her arms around her knees and sobbed.

†

Throwing the paper towel in the first waste bin she saw, Jay carried on walking until she spotted a cab with its sign lit. She gave the driver her address; settled into the back seat and closed her eyes. She could still smell Amanda on her hand and her jeans.

She wasn't proud of the way she'd left. Why did Amanda bring the worst out in her? It had never been like this with Charley. But Charley would have fought back. Amanda never did.

If she could have left before Amanda woke up, the whole thing could have been avoided. She didn't need to be at the clinic before nine thirty but she wanted to take Ritchie for a walk. He'd not had enough exercise the day before. Another reason she couldn't give up the cottage. The terrier loved the sea, the freedom of running along the beach.

Josh wasn't up when she got back to the house. He'd left his dishes in the sink from the night before.

She gave Ritchie his breakfast and set the coffee maker going for a brew before heading up to her bedroom to change out of her jeans and have a quick shower. When she came downstairs, Josh had emerged, sleepy-eyed.

"Sorry about the mess. I was going to clear up before you got home."

"No worries. I'll take Ritchie out. Do you have time for breakfast when we get back?"

"Depends how long you'll be." Ritchie was gazing up at her, head cocked to one side, a hopeful look in his eyes.

"Half an hour tops."

"Pancakes okay for you?"

"Yeah, of course." She gave him a quick hug, then headed for the stairs with Ritchie close on her heels.

The sky was starting to lighten as they reached Kensington Gardens. Dogs were supposed to be kept on their leads, but Jay didn't expect to encounter the park police at this time of the morning. Ritchie raced off as soon as she unclipped his leash. She watched his progress, fingering the plastic bag in her pocket. A cyclist passed her and she smiled to herself. Another person flouting park rules. If she were a park official, Jay thought this would be the ideal time to catch miscreants.

After twenty minutes, she called to Ritchie and he emerged from the bushes a few yards ahead of her.

"Did you do anything in there?" He wagged his tail, then sat for her to reclip his leash on the collar. She handed him his reward and he munched happily as they set off. Jay had a cursory look around the other side of the bush but couldn't see anything.

Back at the house, the smell of freshly brewed coffee overlaid with bacon drifted down the stairs. Josh had only started cooking six years earlier. He hadn't shown any interest before that. Of all the changes in his life, this was the one that had most taken her by surprise.

He was cleaning the frying pan when they arrived in the kitchen. Ritchie had run up the stairs ahead of her and was already sitting by her place at the table. The plate of cooked bacon was well out of his reach.

"Smells wonderful."

"Hm. Only problem with cooking bacon is you'll be smelling it in here for days on end."

"I know. The extractor fan doesn't really do the job." Jay poured coffee into the two mugs on the counter and brought them to the table.

Two pancakes and several rashers of bacon later, Jay pushed her plate aside. "That was fantastic, but I can't eat any more."

"I was going to take a bacon sarnie in to work."

"Good thinking."

"Do you want one?"

"No. Best not torture my clients with the tantalising aroma. I'll need another shower as it is. More coffee?"

"Mm."

She retrieved the coffee pot and brought it to the table. There was just enough for two refills. Jay studied Josh's face as she sat back with the mug in her hands. "What are you thinking?"

"How do you know I'm thinking anything?"

"You have the look of a constipated budgie."

"I do not. And how would you know what one of those looks like?"

"You're deflecting. Come on. What's up?"

"Well, I did have this thought…."

"Ha, I knew it."

"How would you feel about another tattoo?"

Jay put her mug on the table. "For both of us?"

"Well, yeah."

"What's brought this on?"

"I guess, just, you know…."

"Spit it out, son."

"Well, after you get married, you might not be able to…." He looked down at the table, tracing a pattern in the wood. "Sorry. It's probably a stupid idea."

Jay reached over and held his hand. "No, it's not. You've just taken me by surprise. Set up an appointment. Early next week. As long as I have enough notice, I can rearrange some clients. Not possible this week; we have the suit fittings on Friday."

He looked up, tears glistening at the corners of his eyes. "You're the best, you know that?"

"Yes, I am. Don't you forget it." She smiled and let go of his hand. "I'll even wash up if you need to get off."

"Now that's an offer I can't refuse." His answering smile eased the heaviness in her chest that had been with her since leaving Amanda's flat.

"Do you have a design in mind for the tats?"

"Several." He grinned. "I'll email them to you later."

Jay finished washing the dishes before Josh left the house. Another ten minutes and she was ready to leave as well. Ritchie lay in his basket, head between his paws with the soulful look that came into his eyes when he knew he was going to be alone for a while. "Don't lay that guilt trip on me, bud. I know you'll be on the couch as soon as I'm out the door."

Jay always made sure there was a break in her schedule so she could get back during the day to let him out into the garden. Josh could be relied on to take him for a walk when he arrived home from work, usually at least an hour before she did. So the dog had no reason to feel neglected.

She set off for the clinic at a fast pace in an effort to shed some of the calories ingested at breakfast. Waiting for the lights to change at the crossing on Holland Park Avenue, she sent a quick text message to Mo.

†

Mo wondered what Jay had to be sorry about this time. She must have sent her body weight in roses to Amanda Bowen in the last six months. In fact, she could date the first dozen Jay asked her to send from one week after they became officially engaged. Ms Bowen might be a high-flyer in the world of finance, but she seemed utterly clueless in the romance department. Jay's erratic behaviour would have sent any sensible woman running away.

Chapter Three

Josh's eyes lit up as soon as they entered the tailor's shop, and Jay thought this marriage business was worth it just to see that look of joy on his face. Buying a suit was another milestone for Josh. His school uniform didn't count and that had been left behind six years ago. They could have done this sooner but he didn't need a suit for work and the wedding was the first official engagement in his young life.

Perhaps Mo had been right to suggest he would benefit from having a larger family. But she had little experience to draw on. Her parents had died when she was sixteen. Stewart, ten years older, hadn't been around for most of her growing-up years. He made up for it when they were orphaned, though, helping her through those first few difficult years.

She'd had too much loss in her life, too soon. Taking care of Josh had helped her through some of her darkest times. Was she marrying Amanda to fend off the pain of another loss when Josh left to set up his own home? Jay hoped he would find someone to settle down with, but she dreaded the thought of him leaving. As long as he didn't emigrate to Canada or Australia, though, she would cope.

Jay let Josh take the lead in deciding on the colour and style of the suit. Amanda had wanted them to wear traditional morning suits that they could have rented for the occasion, but Jay had resisted.

He had been excited about the wedding from the moment she told him about her engagement.

"Oh wow, Mum. That's great. Did you go down on one knee to propose?"

"No. She asked me."

"Shouldn't it have been the other way around?"

"Why?"

"Well, I mean you're the butch one in the relationship, aren't you?"

"That is such a heterosexist point of view. I thought I'd done a better job of raising you."

Watching Josh interact with the tailor, discussing a particular weave and pattern, Jay was proud of the way he had matured. It hadn't been an easy path for him, but he had met all the challenges in his young life head-on.

The glow of the setting sun coloured the rear-view mirror as Jay turned the Land Rover into the lane. Josh was holding the pizza carton on his lap, with the six-pack of beer between his feet.

"Are you going to tell Amanda about the cottage after you're married?"

"No."

"Why not?"

"I don't know. It's just…well, I don't think she'd understand."

"You're not even giving her a chance to."

Jay parked by the cottage and turned to him. "When did you get so grown up?"

"I'm twenty-four, not twelve."

"So you are." She reached across and ruffled his hair.

"Give over." He pushed her hand away. "You get the bags. I can manage these."

Jay climbed out of the vehicle, glad to stretch her legs after the long drive. Ritchie also struggled out of his comfortable nest on the back seat, looking as stiff as she felt. He recovered quickly, though, and trotted after Josh. *Follow the food* no doubt foremost in his mind.

The bank of clouds hovering over the sea foretold a band of rain coming their way. September had been the wettest month on record, and October looked like it would follow suit. It seemed appropriate that the weather should play its part this weekend, just as it had twenty-three years ago.

How could she begin to explain any of this to Amanda? Why had she kept the cottage? When Charley was officially pronounced dead after the mandatory seven years, she could have sold it and moved on. Breathing in a lungful of the cool breeze, Jay knew the answer, to the second question anyway. This had been Charley's home, the place she always came back to after weeks at sea.

A shout from the cottage brought her back to the present. She walked through the open door and into the open arms of the large bearded man filling the conservatory.

"Dougie," she managed to gasp before he squeezed the breath out of her, dropping both bags onto the floor.

"Hope you don't mind." His deep voice bounced off the walls when he let go of her. "I couldn't make it for July, but I wanted to be here for you this weekend."

"You're always welcome here. You know that."

"What was in the bags? Nothing breakable, I hope."

"Breakfast supplies for tomorrow. Luckily no eggs."

Josh appeared in the doorway. "You guys coming in? The beer's getting warm and so's the pizza."

Dougie scooped the shopping bags off the floor with one hand and followed Jay into the kitchen.

"I'll get the fire started in the living room." Josh disappeared through the far door.

"Go on, Dougie. I'll just put these things away. Won't be long."

Jay smiled to herself as she sorted out the shopping. Bagels, cream cheese, smoked salmon. No harm done there. The juice and milk cartons had miraculously survived the drop as well. Ritchie watched her closely.

"Okay. I haven't forgotten you." She replenished his water bowl from the tap and placed it on the floor. He lapped it up eagerly. While he was occupied, Jay measured out the recommended amount of dry dog food. It didn't look particularly appetising, but she knew that Josh would supplement his diet with real-meat options when she wasn't looking.

Jay checked on the pizza. It was hot enough to be taken out of the oven. She cut it into six manageable slices, grabbed three strips of paper towel, and carried the tray through to the conservatory. Dougie was already on his second beer. He could drink her share, as she planned to start on the whisky.

She had missed Dougie's presence in July. As a tradition born out of shared grief, they would consume a drink or two on the sixth of July, commemorating the Alpha Piper tragedy. Jay lost her brother, and Douglas Rennie lost his lover. Neither he nor Stewart had been able to come out during the time they worked together on the oil rig. Dougie suffered from survivor's guilt even though he could have done nothing to save Stewart or anyone else.

"Ready for a chaser, Dougie?"

"Do you need to ask?"

Jay retrieved the bottle of Dalwhinnie from the cupboard, bought for the occasion, and two tumblers. Josh hadn't acquired a taste for the aqua vitae yet.

With the whisky poured, Jay raised her glass. Dougie raised his, and Josh held up his can of Old Speckled Hen. Each of them said, "Charley," and took a drink. Jay savoured the warmth spreading down her throat and through her torso as the fifteen-year-old Speyside single malt did its work. They sat in silence for a few minutes before Jay broke it. "Have some pizza before it goes cold."

It was a jumbo-size margherita, so the slices she'd cut were huge. Easy enough for Dougie to handle, but she and Josh made more of a mess trying to get it into their mouths. One slice and she was defeated. Josh managed one and a half before giving up. Dougie ate two and finished off Josh's half, but even he couldn't manage the last piece.

Dougie wiped his hands and beard with the paper towel. "Oh hey. I've got a present for you, buddy." For a big man he moved gracefully, getting up and going out to the hallway. He came back and held out a large box to Josh. "They weren't going to let me take this on the plane, but I insisted. Didn't want it getting squashed in the hold. Go on, open it."

"It's not my birthday yet."

"I know. But I couldn't resist getting you this. All the dudes in Alberta have one."

Josh opened the lid cautiously. His eyes widened and a radiant smile appeared. "Oh my God! A Stetson." He lifted the hat out and placed it on his head.

"Not like that, you pillock." Dougie reached over and adjusted the brim.

"Mum, you've got to take a pic. This is so lit." He pulled his phone out of his back pocket and handed it to her. "Thanks, Dougie."

Jay tapped in the code on his phone and took the picture. "It may be all the rage in Alberta, but I don't know where you're going to wear it here."

"Well, yeah. A few more accessories might be needed. Boots, chaps...." Josh grinned at Dougie.

"A horse."

"That too."

Josh took his phone back and fiddled with it. The photo was no doubt now on Instagram or whatever other popular app young people used to share all the details of their lives.

After listening to Dougie's most recent tales of life in the Canadian Wild West of Alberta while finishing her drink, Jay excused herself, ready for an early night.

†

It had been staring her in the face and she hadn't seen it. *Call yourself a journalist.* Tess wondered what else her parents knew. She could have saved herself a trip out to the wilds of the Norfolk coast.

She was seven when her Auntie Char stopped visiting. Her mum only told her that she had gone away. After a time, Tess stopped asking when she would be coming back. The first few years, though, she'd been upset that the generous flow of Christmas and birthday presents had ceased. But then life took over and there were other disappointments to overcome in the ensuing years.

"Are we going in?"

Tess released her seat belt. "Yeah, sorry. Miles away." She gave Alice what she hoped was a reassuring smile.

"Is everything okay? With us, I mean. You've been a bit distant for a while now."

"Of course we're okay. It's…it's just this story I'm working on." Tess leaned in for a kiss.

Alice moved out of range and opened her door. "If you say so."

Great. Now I'm a crap girlfriend on top of everything else. Tess removed the car keys from the ignition and got out. By the time she'd collected the bottle of wine from the back seat and locked up, Alice was already turning into the gate of Tess's parents' house. She hurried to catch up and arrived just as the door opened and Alice was greeted enthusiastically by Donna.

Up until Tess's late teens, her parents had been Mum and Mummy. After her first sex-education class at school, she came home and asked which one of them had carried her in their womb. Neither of them could look her in the eye. Donna looked at Cheryl, and Tess could see the struggle going on in their heads. Surely they would have been prepared to answer this question at some point. They had, she knew now, been somewhat economical with the truth when they gave her the facts of life, her life. She had started to refer to them in her head as Parent One and Parent Two. Although really they should be relegated to Three and Four once she knew she'd been adopted.

Tess closed the door behind her. Alice and Donna had already disappeared, but she could hear their voices in the living room. She carried on down the hallway to the kitchen at the back of the house. Cheryl was there bending down to check on the roast in the oven.

"Hi, Mum." Hard to break the habit of a lifetime. Until she'd asked the fatal question, she'd always thought Cheryl was her biological mother. Tess winced when she thought of how she'd reacted to the news that Cheryl wasn't.

"Did you pay her to have me?"

"No. That would have been illegal," Cheryl said calmly. "We did help her out with travel expenses and some other research-related costs."

"And before you were born, she stayed here during holidays when she wasn't at uni or out at sea," Donna added.

Cheryl closed the oven door and stood. "Hi, sweetie." She pulled her into a hug, and Tess let the parental warmth envelop her, as it always did. Whatever the circumstances of her birth, she had never lacked a loving home environment.

†

Awake long before the usual pre-dawn raucous chorus from the seagulls heralding the return of the night-fishing trawlers, Jay shifted around in her bed trying to get comfortable. She had been tired from the long drive from the city and the effects of the whisky, so sleep had come quickly. But it wasn't going to return any time soon.

The day ahead would be filled with memories, not all of them good. But she felt better about it with Dougie being here. Although she could talk to Josh about his mother, he didn't remember her. He was only eleven months old when the boat sank, changing both their lives irrevocably.

Finally, giving in to the fact she wasn't going to get back to sleep, Jay got out of bed. She pulled on a T-shirt and sweatpants before leaving the bedroom in case she encountered Dougie on her way to the bathroom.

When she poked her head around the sitting-room door, her visitor was fast asleep on the sofa with Ritchie curled under one arm. If they'd stayed up talking and drinking, she could guess Josh wouldn't be feeling too lively for a while yet, either. She wasn't sure what Ritchie's excuse was. Maybe he'd gorged on the last slice of pizza.

Jay added a sweatshirt and trainers to her outfit and slipped out through the conservatory. The hint of a red sky was making an appearance as she set off for her morning run down to the beach and back.

She lingered for a while, walking out to meet the receding waves, leaving a trail of prints in the glistening sand. More times than she could count in those first few years, she had stood in this same spot hoping for a miracle. But this wasn't a Bond film. Her lost love wasn't going to come wading out of the sea clad in a white bikini.

Looking after Josh had stopped her from taking her own life. At first she hadn't thought she could cope with caring for a baby, but she wasn't going to give up on the child. He was all she had left of Charley.

As the sky brightened in the east, casting its glow over the sea, she scanned the shoreline in both directions. No sign of any stranded, distressed seals. She would make a more diligent survey when the three of them came out later for their annual vigil, each silently remembering Charley.

The smell of freshly brewed coffee met her nostrils as she opened the door to the conservatory. Dougie was in the kitchen preparing their breakfast of toasted bagels with cream cheese and smoked salmon.

"Morning. Thought I'd get started. You don't mind, do you?"

"Not at all." Jay picked up one of the full glasses of orange juice on the table and drank it down. "I'll have a quick shower, if the bathroom's free."

"The boy hasn't stirred, so it's all yours."

Refreshed from her run and the shower, Jay felt ready to take on the day, the effects of her lack of sleep washed away.

"Where's Ritchie?" She accepted the mug of coffee from Dougie and inhaled the life-enhancing aroma before taking a sip.

"By the fire. I let him out to do his business, but he didn't stay out long."

Jay sat down at the table. "Did you and Josh stay up much later?"

"Maybe an hour or so." He handed her a plate with a toasted bagel on it.

They ate in silence. Something Jay had always appreciated about her brother's lover. He didn't feel the need to talk all the time. He managed to eat two bagels to her one. Leaving the breakfast things for Josh to use when he showed up, they took their second mugs of coffee in to the conservatory. Jay angled the vertical blinds to block out the full force of the sun now rising above the horizon.

"Are you sure you really want to do this?" Dougie asked.

"Today? Yes, of course."

"No, I meant the wedding."

Jay sighed. "What's Josh been saying?"

"Just that you don't seem too enthusiastic about it. He seems to have a soft spot for Amanda. Doesn't want to see her get hurt."

"God, the sooner he gets a steady girlfriend, the better."

"Why?"

"So he can stop analysing my love life."

"Do you think he will...?" Dougie hesitated.

She knew what he was thinking; they'd hashed it over a number of times. Jay finished the sentence. "Find someone who will accept him as he is?" She squeezed Dougie's knee. "In time. Luckily he doesn't seem anxious about it. He's only twenty-four, after all."

"People are married with three kids at that age."

"We weren't."

"No, but...." Dougie stopped as Josh stepped through the doorway carrying a heaped plate and a mug of coffee.

"You two look guilty as hell. Talking about me?"

"Nothing bad." Dougie smiled at him. "We were talking about the wedding plans. When will I get to see you dressed up?"

"Fitting's next week. Right, Mum?" He took a big bite out of the bagel.

"Yes. Will you be back in town then, Dougie?"

"Probably the week after. I've got some meetings in London after I get back from other visits, Edinburgh and Brighton."

†

A traditional Sunday lunch on Saturday. Tess's parents had changed the day when they took up golf. The club's competitions were on Sundays. She had never thought of either of them as particularly sporty, but they had taken to the game with great enthusiasm, which hadn't wavered in ten years. Donna was even going to be Lady Captain at the club for the second time when the new season started up in April.

Tess let the conversation at the table drift over her. Alice was doing a good job of entertaining them with tales of her new job as a police community support officer. A failure on Tess's part when she'd dented her initial excitement, telling Alice it was a step above traffic warden and that real police officers referred to the PCSOs as "plastics". The uniform was pretty cool, though.

A kick on her shin brought her back to the present with Donna saying, "We'll clear the table and bring coffee through." Tess glared at Alice, then stood to collect plates and follow Parent Two into the kitchen.

"What's up, love? Are you and Alice having problems?" Donna started rinsing the dishes for Tess to place in the dishwasher.

"No."

"Well, what, then? You were miles away throughout the meal."

Donna dried her hands and switched on the coffee maker. Tess knew that Cheryl would have set it up beforehand. Their routine never varied. She finished stacking the plates and stood.

"I went to Norfolk last weekend."

"Yes, we missed you. Alice said you were working on a project."

"You could say that. I met Jay Reid." Tess didn't miss the flicker of recognition in Donna's eyes. "I thought it was time someone wrote a biography about England's greatest female tennis player."

"Oh, well, yes. I remember her. She retired from the game early, though, didn't she?"

"Yeah."

There was real fear in Donna's face now. "Did she tell you why?"

"Not in so many words."

Donna turned away to watch the dark liquid dripping into the coffee pot. "This is almost ready. Can you take the tray through?"

Something else Cheryl had prepared earlier. Her thirty-five years as a science teacher meant she always had her laboratory set up in advance of the lesson, on the domestic front as well as in the classroom.

"Why didn't you tell me?"

"We never met Jay. Char told us when she started seeing her, but we were sworn to secrecy about their relationship. Jay had a reputation as a player, in more than one sense, so the media hadn't caught on. Char stopped coming round about a year before the accident. It was her idea to tell you she was doing research in Antarctica. So, you see, there's not much we could tell you. We weren't surprised to hear Jay Reid stopped playing. I'm sure she knew about your existence, but she didn't contact us. And we weren't going to out Char posthumously."

"Why would anyone care?"

"If you'd been born a few decades earlier you wouldn't be asking that. The eighties and early nineties were a difficult time for homosexuals, gay men particularly."

"Oh, you mean with AIDS. I've read about that but surely it didn't affect lesbians in the same way." Tess was stopped by the look on Donna's face. "Shit. You mean Stewart Reid was gay. And he was my dad?"

Donna offered a mirthless smile. "The sperm donor, yes. Says something about nature versus nurture, doesn't it? You didn't stand a chance of not being gay. If you'd turned out to be heterosexual we would have wondered what we did wrong."

Alice burst through the kitchen doorway. "Hey, we're dying of caffeine deprivation out here. Is it ready?" Seemingly oblivious to the tension in the room, she grabbed the coffee pot. "Bring the tray, Tess."

Numbed by the new revelation about her parentage, Tess picked up the tray and followed her out. Cheryl looked up as they entered the lounge. "Oh good. I thought maybe I'd forgotten to set up the coffee maker."

†

Amanda couldn't concentrate on the menu choices, but it didn't matter. She always had the same thing. "Tuna melt on ciabatta. No fries."

"I'll have the avocado toast. With fries." Lynne waited for the server to walk away before adding, "I don't have a sleek wedding dress to fit into. My bridesmaid outfit has an elasticated waist." She leant forward, elbows on the table. "So what's eating you? It can't be just because your fiancée has disappeared for the weekend. She does that on a regular basis."

"No, it's...well, maybe. I wish I knew where she goes. Do you think she has another woman somewhere?"

"It's a bit late to be asking that. You're getting married in less than three weeks." Lynne leant back in her chair. "Anyway, I don't get that vibe off Jay. She's a straight arrow if you ask me."

"Nothing straight about her." Amanda smiled for the first time since they'd arrived at the café.

"Hey, I don't want to know about your sex life. Well, maybe I do, since mine's non-existent at the moment."

A flush of desire shot through Amanda, as it always did when thoughts of sex with Jay came to mind. Her lover had more than made up for the way she'd left her on Tuesday morning with another night of passion on Thursday. Jay's hot episodes were more frequent than her cold ones. When they were married, Amanda was looking forward to spending seven nights a week with her instead of the two or sometimes, blissfully, three they managed now. She tried hard not to be jealous of Josh. And it was ridiculous to feel any animosity toward a dog. But she often resented the time Jay spent with her son and Ritchie. That would change after the wedding.

"Earth to Amanda." Lynne waved a hand in front of her face.

She sighed. "My dad's arriving this week and wants to have dinner with us."

"Oh wow. I would love to be a fly on the wall for that meeting."

"I'm not sure it's a good idea. But he insisted."

"Don't worry. I'm sure Jay has plenty of experience with dealing with men like him."

"Sexist, homophobic, misogynist, Neanderthal...."

"That's probably an insult to Neanderthals. They were more advanced intellectually than they've formerly been given credit for. Did you know—?"

"I'm sure it's a fascinating topic, Professor. But I don't need an anthropology lecture right now."

Their food arrived, and for a few minutes silence reigned at the table.

"What about your mother?" Lynne took a sip of her mineral water. "Doesn't she want to meet Jay before the wedding?"

"No. I'm inconveniencing her as it is. She had tickets for a Rossini opera in Venice. I'm sure she's seen *The Barber of Seville* a dozen times, at least. I think she's hoping for a French train strike so she can have an excuse for not coming."

"Why don't you two just go to a registry office? I mean, Jay doesn't have any family. Apart from her son. So it could just be the four of us."

Amanda took one of Lynne's fries and stuck it in her mouth. "Because," she said slowly after she'd swallowed, "I want it to be special. To mean something more than signatures on a piece of paper. Ideally I would have liked a church wedding. But Jay refused to consider it. She objects to the church's stance on gays and women bishops."

"I totally agree with her on that. But the ceremony at Dartmouth House will be pretty special."

"Yes. Although it was my second choice. I would have liked One Canada Square at Canary Wharf. But it was already booked."

"Probably would have been too big for the number of guests. The Mayfair venue is better suited to a small group.

I'm sure you've got it sorted, but is there anything you need me to do ahead of time?"

"No. It's all under control. Just be there for me on the day. I'm not sure I can rely on either of my parents to do that."

"And I know you've got the honeymoon booked. Although I had thought you might be going somewhere more exotic like Hawaii or the Seychelles."

"My first choice was Hawaii. But Jay said she couldn't take more than a week off work. So it didn't seem worth it to fly all that way and feel jet-lagged for most of the week. Anyway it's still quite warm in Corsica this time of year. And I've never been there before."

Lynne grinned at her. "Come on. You don't go on a honeymoon to do sightseeing. You could have just booked a hotel here for all the amount of time you'll spend out of the bedroom."

Amanda felt the flush through her whole body. "Damn it, Lynne. I feel like a teenager in heat just thinking about it."

"She's really got you hooked, hasn't she? I only met her once. I mean, I can see the attraction, but it didn't go any deeper than that for me."

"Good. Otherwise I'd be looking for another bridesmaid."

†

After saying goodbye to Amanda outside the restaurant, Lynne continued her Saturday programme with her regular visit to the British Library. She stopped to gaze at the impressive sight of the King's Library rising up through the middle of the building, a wonderful legacy from George III, the so-called "mad king". Lynne subscribed to the view, along with many other scholars, that the poor man suffered from a mental illness that went untreated. Mad or not, he had left the nation a wonderful collection of books and pamphlets gathered from all corners of the world.

She settled down in the Reading Room with the archived document she'd requested online earlier in the week.

Although she had dismissed the idea of Jay Reid seeing someone else when she was with Amanda, the woman was hiding something. What were these mystery weekends about? Amanda was so besotted with Jay that she wasn't thinking beyond their next sexual encounter. Her best friend was intelligent in many respects, but observation of human behaviour wasn't one of her strong points.

Lynne, however, was an anthropologist. It was an occupational obsession with her, watching people, analysing the little details that made up everyday lives. Researching Jay's tennis career had proven a dead end. And wasn't relevant, Lynne surmised. So she'd started at the other end, with Jay's current occupation. Amanda had only told her that Jay managed a physical-therapy clinic called CSC in Notting Hill. That was easy enough to find online. Only when she probed deeper did she find out what the acronym stood for. The name Charlotte Summersbridge hovered on the edge of her consciousness.

The disappearance of a marine-mammal research vessel, *RV Caspian*, somewhere in the North Sea was all but forgotten. No bodies had been retrieved. But, like the old king, Charlotte Summersbridge left a legacy. Her doctoral thesis was considered to be the definitive analysis of PDV in the European seal population.

Lynne opened the bound treatise in front of her. Phocine Distemper Virus. Charlotte's observations and conclusions were based on the 1988 outbreak. As well as her scientific data, she'd also included extracts from media reports at the time which likened PDV to AIDS. Cause unknown. What made Charlotte's paper readable was her obvious empathy with the subjects of her study. She cared deeply about the suffering of the seals.

As she walked home from the library, Lynne tried to come up with a reason ex-tennis player Jay Reid would have named her clinic after a marine biologist. There had to be a link and, she suspected, a very personal one. But as she'd already discovered, Charlotte Summersbridge had left virtually no digital footprint. Only an academic trail that consisted of published reports, her master's degree dissertation, and the thesis Lynne had just read. No co-authors to track down.

She put the kettle on as soon as she got in. Her two cats, Slinky and Babs, greeted her with piteous cries. "I've only been gone five hours. You can't be starving already." Their matching expressions said otherwise, pleading looks that she couldn't ignore. "All right. I saved some chicken from last night."

With the cats eagerly devouring their snack, Lynne took her mug of tea into the sitting room and booted up her laptop. The Zoological Society's website gave more current information about seals and the fact there had been another major PDV outbreak in 2002 leading to the deaths of over half the seal population in the North Sea region. Further searches led to the fact that volunteers were deployed around the coasts to check on stranded seals. Something else she learned: seals regularly "hauled-out" onto beaches to rest and digest food, where whales, dolphins, and porpoises didn't "beach" themselves under normal circumstances.

Lynne followed this by looking up seal sanctuaries and their locations around the UK. The one in Norfolk was probably the most accessible from London. It was just possible, she thought, that if Jay Reid did have a personal connection with the deceased Charlotte—she felt she was on first-name terms with the biologist now—they could have property on the Norfolk coast. Charlotte would likely have wanted to be close to her subjects. Was this where Jay spent her weekends? It would be a half-day drive but perfect for a complete getaway from the city.

†

Ritchie dashed ahead of them, barking at an incoming wave and leaping out of the way before the water reached his paws.

They were an odd-looking procession. Dougie carried the portable windbreak and two of the folding chairs; Josh followed with the other chair and the picnic hamper. He'd wanted to wear his Stetson, but the gusty breeze had dissuaded him. Jay brought up the rear, trying to keep the two bottles of champagne upright, clutching them close to her body to make sure they didn't get shaken up too much.

The beach was deserted. This time of year there wasn't much traffic anyway. Only the odd twitcher now and again. When they reached their usual spot, Dougie set up the windbreak. Once the chairs were unfolded, the hamper and bottles safely deposited nearby, Jay stood between the two men. With linked arms they gazed out to sea. Ritchie knew his part in the ritual and joined them, lying down next to Josh and resting his head on his paws.

Jay closed her eyes; so many memories of Charley tumbled through her mind. But one that stood out clearly was the scene in the hotel room in the aftermath of her Wimbledon win. The first time Charley said I love you. Winning one of the tennis world's greatest prizes couldn't match that feeling of joy when Charley whispered those three words in her ear. Amanda had said the same words to her many times over the last six months. But they didn't have the same effect. Jay shook her head, opening her eyes to concentrate on the sea. Today was about Charley. Amanda had no place here.

There was no set time for their meditations. They all seemed to know when it was done and broke the link together. No words were needed as they set about the task of unpacking the picnic hamper, and opening and pouring the champagne to raise a silent toast to the woman who had affected all their lives deeply.

The cottage felt empty after Dougie had gone. Ritchie was asleep by the fire, tired out from the morning's excursion. Jay thought Josh had gone into his bedroom but then saw that the attic hatch was open. He'd pulled the ladder up, an indication he wanted to be on his own.

Jay pottered about in the kitchen, tidying up the breakfast debris and the remains of the picnic. She had offered to drive Dougie to King's Lynn, but he'd insisted on taking a taxi. Whatever his plans were, he wasn't sharing. Having spent most of the past year in Alberta, he no doubt had some catching up to do with other friends.

"But it's quiz night at the sex tent," Josh had exclaimed when Dougie told them he wasn't staying for another night. The Sextant was their local pub, just over a mile away in the village. Some incomers had started a petition a few years back to have the pub name changed to The Anchor. But the landlord had stood firm and told the instigators that if they didn't like it, they could take their custom elsewhere. That would have meant a journey of ten miles to the next drinking establishment, so The Sextant remained, proud of its nautical heritage.

With the light starting to fade, Jay stoked up the fire, adding another log. They would have to make a decision on whether they were staying in to eat or heading down to the pub. She called up to Josh and getting no answer, pulled the cord to release the ladder.

He was huddled in the small space between the trunk and wall, hugging his knees to his chest. The old photo album lay open by his side. She couldn't see his expression in the gloom, but she didn't need to. Jay had spent many hours up here herself in the same position. The trunk held Charley's clothes and the few items of jewellery she had owned. And the album of photographs from their early days together.

"Come on down, love. If you don't feel like going out we've got enough food in for a meal."

Josh lifted his head. "Dougie finished off the beer, though."

"Ah. Well, better get a move on, then. Or the best seats will be taken." She withdrew her head from the hatch and backed down the narrow metal steps.

They rarely competed well in the pub quiz. Without Dougie's superior knowledge on any sports-related questions, they were generally pleased if they didn't finish last.

Josh and Ritchie slept for the first part of the journey back to London on Sunday. After their pit stop at Mildenhall, Josh offered to drive the rest of the way, but Jay knew he'd drunk more than she had at The Sextant and she felt refreshed from the injection of caffeine and sugar at the café.

Chapter Four

Secrecy and lies. Tess was like a terrier with a bone when she was on the trail of a good story. A quality that helped tremendously when tracking down other people's stories. Alice's observation when she finally told her what she was trying to do had hit home.

"Now you know how it feels. Maybe you should leave it alone."

"It's all right for you. You know who your parents are."

"So do you. Donna and Cheryl."

"It's not the same. They adopted me. Paid for me."

"Look. They wanted you. Loved you. Even though you're a pain in the arse, they still do. A lot of babies don't get that."

"It wasn't even a proper surrogacy, though. None of their eggs were involved. I'm the product of Charlotte Summersbridge and Stewart Reid."

"Sounds like they were both very fine people. So what's your problem?"

Tess had left it alone then. Their Sunday had passed off peacefully, meeting two other friends for brunch, then binge-watching three episodes of *The Crown* on Netflix.

As Monday wore on, trying and failing to concentrate on the story her editor expected her to finish by six o'clock, she couldn't shake off the feeling she was missing something. On Google Maps, Tess brought up the address she'd memorised. Social climbers in that part of Notting Hill often referred it to as North Kensington.

With a decision made, she buckled down and made the deadline with just seconds to spare. After a tense wait that felt like hours but was only five minutes, her editor emailed her back with a few minor amendments. Leaving the building at six thirty, she only hoped Jay Reid didn't work a nine-to-five, or even ten-to-six day.

Tess liked her flexible hours mainly because she could miss the commuting crush. The tube trains would still be crowded at this time, and if it was a bright summer's evening, she would have walked, enjoying a stroll through Hyde Park and Kensington Gardens. But a dark October early evening wasn't tempting. Bracing herself for an uncomfortable ten-minute journey, she joined the scrum jostling for position on the platform. It was a wonder, she thought, that more people didn't end up on the tracks in front of oncoming trains. She had to let the first train go but just managed to squeeze into a space by the door of the second one.

†

Jay finished typing up her notes on the last client of the day. Although people arrived at the clinic for various treatments, she discouraged her staff from referring to them as patients. Most of them came for physiotherapy sessions after hip or knee operations. Her own specialty wasn't generally recognised by the medical community as a valid treatment. Much as acupuncture had been scorned when it first started to be practiced outside China, it would take time for cranial-sacral therapy to be recognised as anything more than some kind of mystical witchcraft. In less enlightened times, she would probably have been burned at the stake.

The woman she had just spent an hour with who had come in barely able to stand upright from the pain in her back and legs had practically run out of the building claiming to have been "cured." Jay didn't believe in miracles, but she was pleased with the result.

She switched off her computer and picked up her phone. There was one message from Amanda. It just said, *Dinner with dad Claridges 8:15, don't be late.* Jay sighed. Meeting her soon-to-be father-in-law was something she wasn't looking forward to. She certainly didn't want to sit through a three-hour-long multi-course tasting menu if that was the only option. Having googled his name, she expected him to arrive wearing a white sheet, his political views appearing to be on the extreme far right of the spectrum. Did he know his daughter was marrying a woman?

Seven o'clock now, so no need to rush. She was caught up with her work, having taken the morning off to go to the tattoo parlour with Josh. The memory of their shared experience would sustain her through this dinner engagement and fending off questions from Amanda later when she saw the redness surrounding the new image on her skin. It was only partially done. They were going back next week to have colours added. Resisting the urge to scratch the newly disturbed area of skin on her upper arm, she checked her diary for the next day.

A knock on the door was followed by it opening quickly. Ross Cooper, the head physio, stood there looking red-faced. "Sorry, boss. But she insisted on seeing you. I did tell her to make an appointment."

The young woman who pushed past him was instantly recognisable. Tess perched on the edge of the visitor's chair, piercing her with a look that Jay knew only too well.

"Thanks, Ross. It's okay. Have a good evening."

When the door closed, Jay sat back and waited. It had always worked with Charley. Whatever she'd done to merit the angry stare would soon be revealed.

"You knew, didn't you?"

"Knew what?"

"Knew who I am. Made me drive all the way to sodding Norfolk and didn't say a word about her or your brother."

"I didn't know, until I saw you."

"You're my aunt." Tess's angry tone hadn't lessened.

Jay looked at the ceiling and counted to ten before she said anything she might regret. "Biologically speaking, yes." She brought her gaze back to the younger woman's intense glare. "Have you talked to your parents about this?"

"Yes. But they can't tell me much. I only found out this weekend that your brother was the sperm donor and that he was gay."

"What does that have to do with the price of eggs?"

"I would just like to know more about my biological parents. And you're the only person who knew them both intimately."

A silence hung between them as Jay considered her response, wavering between anger and sorrow. She could see that Tess wasn't going to give up easily. Her expression held the same fire and intensity she'd so often seen on Charley's face. After a few deep breaths, she managed to say calmly, "I lost two people I loved. Intimately."

"I know, but...."

"But, if I'm going to talk to you about them, and it's still a big if, then I have to know I'm talking to my niece, not an investigative journalist."

"It's quite a story. People will only have the deepest sympathy for all the losses in your life. First, your parents at a young age, then both your brother and your lover in extreme circumstances."

"Yes. A right little misery memoir that would a publishing sensation, I'm sure. But it's not going to happen, Tess." It wasn't just her memories she wanted to protect. Jay couldn't expose Josh to the media glare. Thankfully, Tess wasn't aware of his existence. Not yet, anyway.

Tess didn't drop her gaze. Jay looked away first and knew she'd lost a point. Fifteen-love to her opponent.

"Look. I've got a dinner engagement tonight. But we could meet up later in the week."

"You're not putting me off, are you? And I'm not driving to the arse-end of Norfolk again."

"Hm. Too bad. You could learn a lot there."

"You're not serious!"

"No. Just messing." Jay opened the diary on her phone. "Thursday evening would be okay. Here at the clinic."

"Great." Tess didn't even consult her own calendar. "What time?"

"Six thirty."

"Okay. Thank you." Tess stood. "Sorry about barging in on you."

"No problem. Just don't make a habit of it."

After the girl left, Jay sat for a few minutes, wondering why she'd given in so easily. Was it just the unsettling resemblance to Charley? She lived with that every day through Josh. The unwelcome thought came to her that Mo was probably right. She needed to let her memories of Charley go. Twenty-three years was a long time to hang on to a ghost.

†

"I'm sure she'll be here any minute." Amanda could see the signs. Her father's blood pressure was rising. "She may have had trouble getting a taxi. The rain's started again."

"Five more minutes, then we'll start without her. Damned thoughtless, if you ask me."

Jay walked through the door of the restaurant before her father could develop his theme on people who were late any further.

"Well, you can relax. She's here now." Amanda smiled, relief coursing through her as Jay threaded her way easily past the other tables to reach them.

"Sorry to keep you waiting; a client came in just as I was leaving. One of my regulars, so I couldn't turn him away." Jay extended her right hand. "Pleased to meet you, Mr Bowen."

He ignored her and picked up his menu. "Good. We can order now."

Amanda tapped his arm. "Dad, please...."

"Let's just get on with it, shall we?"

Jay remained standing. Amanda knew the signs well; the fuse once lit didn't take long to ignite. "If you can't show me any respect, you could at least make an effort for your daughter's sake."

A grunt was all she got in response as he continued to peruse the menu, although Amanda knew he'd chosen what he wanted minutes after they arrived.

"Fine. Enjoy your meal, sir." Jay laid a heavy emphasis on the last word, turned on her heel and walked out.

Whatever she'd expected from their meeting, Amanda had thought they might at least have got through the main course.

"Are we having red or white?"

Amanda replaced her napkin on the table as calmly as she could manage. "You have whatever you want. You're dining on your own now."

He made no attempt to stop her as she picked up her handbag and stood. When she looked back from the entrance to the restaurant, he was talking to the sommelier.

Amanda made her way outside and lingered under the awning, hesitating to venture out into the misty drizzle. Jay reached her side at the same time as a taxi pulled up.

"Come on, love. Let's go home."

Hearing the word *home* from Jay brought a rush of joy mingled with relief through her entire body. When Jay gave the driver the address to the flat, Amanda's happiness level soared. Her father's disapproval of her chosen partner faded into the background. She snuggled against Jay, enjoying the feel of her arm around her shoulders.

†

Deuce

Jay had been prepared to play nicely with Amanda's father. She didn't know how she'd managed to control herself after his overt snub. In another location, she might have given in to the temptation to spit on his bald patch. However, Claridge's wasn't the place to cause a scene that would probably be recorded by another diner and all over social media before she'd left the building.

She wondered, briefly, as she stood on the pavement, whether Amanda would stay to try to placate her parent. But she'd hardly had time to realise she was getting wet waiting for the taxi she'd ordered when Amanda came out.

Neither of them spoke until they were inside the flat. Amanda hung her coat up in the closet by the door and held her hand out for Jay's jacket.

"Are you hungry?" Amanda placed her shoes on the mat. As she stood on the parquet flooring in her stockings, her head only reached the top of Jay's shoulders.

"Hungry for you, yes." She bent her head to kiss Amanda's slightly parted lips, inviting her in.

The way her lover's body responded to the slightest touch never failed to ignite Jay's carnal instincts. Giving Amanda what she clearly craved was easy, but Jay was often left feeling dissatisfied. Something that had never troubled her when making love with Charley.

Their stomachs growled in unison. Jay put her hand on Amanda's belly, feeling it under her fingers, still trembling from her last orgasm. "Guess we need feeding."

"I don't think I can move."

Jay rose on one elbow, leaning over her. "Well, I can." She glanced at the bedside clock. "Time to get up anyway."

"There's not much in if you want something to eat here. You have a choice of baked beans on toast, or cereal, or both."

"A coffee will do for starters. I'll pick something up on my way to the clinic." Jay sat up and stretched before getting out of bed. After a quick trip to the bathroom, she returned to the bedroom to retrieve her clothes from the floor where they lay in a haphazard pile, hastily discarded the night before.

"Aren't you going to have a shower?" Amanda had pulled the duvet close around her body, only her head showing.

"I can take one at work. I have a change of clothes there." Jay finished dressing and walked through to the kitchen and switched the kettle on. She then texted Josh to remind him to take Ritchie for a walk.

Amanda's kitchen had all modern conveniences but one. Jay located the coffee-filter papers and tin of ground coffee. She knew there was a cafetière lurking in one of the cupboards, but Amanda claimed she didn't like the taste of the coffee from it. The first thing she would buy if she moved in would be a coffee maker.

But could she live here? Tower Bridge loomed outside the window. A view a lot of people would find charming. Jay felt oppressed by it. The garden at the back of the mews house was small, but it was an inviting patch of greenery. A private and peaceful space in the midst of the bustling city. Staying in Amanda's flat for any length of time gave her a feeling of claustrophobia, which she couldn't adequately explain when the views from the living room offered an expansive vista of the Thames to the west.

Jay waited for the water to drip through into one mug. When that was filled, she reset the cone with another filter paper, spooned in the fresh grounds, and waited for the kettle to come to a boil again. By the time the second mug was ready, Amanda had come into the kitchen, wrapped in a towel, her hair still wet from the shower

Jay opened the fridge and placed the carton of milk on the counter. She drank her coffee black, but Amanda liked a splash of the white stuff in hers. Jay handed her the mug.

"Thanks, babe." She took a sip. "Sure you can't stay for something to eat?"

"Sorry. Full day of appointments." Her phone buzzed. A message from Josh with a thumbs-up emoji. Jay took several big gulps of coffee. "I need to get going. Catch you later." She gave Amanda a quick peck on the cheek and made her escape.

Pausing on the pavement to catch her breath from running down the stairwell, she wondered why it always felt like a release when she left the confines of the apartment. On the ground she didn't feel threatened by the presence of the bridge. It was just another part of the familiar London landscape.

†

Amanda stood at the window watching the river traffic. After the joys of lovemaking during the night and in the early morning, Jay's abrupt departure left her feeling empty. A ringing sound broke the silence and she hurried into the bedroom to retrieve her phone. The brief flicker of hope died when she saw Lynne's name on the screen.

"Hi. Hope I didn't wake you."

"No, I'm up."

"How did the meeting with Daddy go?"

"It was a disaster. Jay was a bit late getting to the restaurant and he wouldn't look at her. So she walked out."

"Oh no! What did you do?"

"Well, he was going to carry on as if nothing had happened. When I left he was ordering wine."

"You left as well?"

"Yes. But Jay was waiting for me outside. We had a good night."

"You sound a bit down. I guess she's not there now."

"No." Amanda tried to keep the bitterness out of her voice. But Lynne knew her too well to be fooled.

"There's more to a relationship than sex. It's not too late to call off the wedding."

Amanda was on the verge of tears now. "I can't. I want her more than ever."

Lynne's sigh was magnified through the phone connection.

"I know what you're going to say. I've fallen into the trap of thinking she'll change once we're married."

"Exactly. So why go through with it?"

"Because I love her."

Another sigh. "Look, there's something I've found out. Can you meet me for lunch or after work today?"

"What is it? Can you tell me now?"

"I'd rather not over the phone."

Wondering what Lynne wanted to tell her kept Amanda on tenterhooks all day. Her colleagues knew about the upcoming wedding and gave her some leeway when she zoned out at her desk. Her supervisor smiled at her indulgently and gave her the tedious job of stuffing envelopes. Being given such a menial junior task would have irritated Amanda on any other day, but she was happy to be

Deuce

able to spend the time daydreaming. Her favourite was the one where she was walking up the aisle in her wedding dress towards a smiling Jay. With the vows and rings exchanged, they would kiss and walk back down the aisle together to begin their life of wedded bliss.

†

Drink in hand, Lynne led the way to a dark corner of the pub, where they could settle in to comfortable chairs with a degree of privacy.

"Has Jay ever mentioned a Charlotte Summersbridge?"

Amanda's eyes widened. "Is she the other woman or a previous girlfriend?"

"I take that as a no. She possibly was a previous girlfriend."

"Do you think Jay still sees her?"

"Only in her dreams. She's dead and has been for the last twenty-three years."

"Why do you think there's a connection?"

Lynne sipped her gin and tonic and placed the glass carefully on the table before answering. "The name of Jay's clinic. CSC. Did you ever wonder what the initials stand for?"

"Something to do with that therapy treatment she does…cranial sacral what's-it…oh."

"Yes, oh. It's named after Charlotte Summersbridge. Now, I think that's odd, if there's no link. She wouldn't have picked that name randomly."

Amanda took a large swig of her white wine. "Who was she? How did she die?"

"Well, that's rather interesting. She was a marine biologist and her specialist subject was diseased seals."

"What?"

"I won't bore you with all the details but she was something of a rising star in the marine-mammal community. She died, along with the entire crew, when their research vessel sank in the North Sea. The boat was never found and neither were the bodies."

"Seals." Amanda closed her eyes briefly. When she opened them again, she leant forward eagerly. "Jay has a tattoo, on her left arm, just below her shoulder. I think it's a seal. And she's had another one done recently. On the other arm. I saw it this morning when she got of bed. But I didn't have a chance to ask her about it."

"Hm. More food for thought. Do you want another drink?"

"Yes, I think I do."

Lynne made her way to the bar and waited for the barman to finish pulling two pints for the man in front of her. When it was her turn to order, she had to shout to make herself heard above the noise of all the patrons enthusiastically enjoying the release from their working days. As she looked back at their table while she waited, Amanda was staring at her phone. If she thought she could summon up a call from her lover by wishful thinking, Lynne could tell her it wasn't going to happen. Jay, to her knowledge, had never initiated anything in the relationship. For it to have lasted this long, she had to be sensational in bed.

Lynne paid for the drinks and pushed back through the crowd to the table. Amanda had taken a large gulp from her glass even before she'd reseated herself.

"Anyway, the seal business got me thinking." Lynne sipped at her G and T. "This mystery place Jay goes to on weekends could be by the sea. Following the Charlotte connection, there are seal sanctuaries situated around the coasts and she would probably have wanted to be close to one of them."

Lynne watched Amanda's face as she mulled this over. At one time, she thought she had a chance to be more than a friend. But she left it too long and when she'd finally gathered the courage to say something, Amanda had met Jay Reid and fallen hopelessly, to Lynne's mind, in love.

From the ups and downs of the relationship that she'd witnessed, Lynne couldn't see the marriage lasting more than a few months. Although she didn't want to see Amanda's heart shattered, she was willing to stick around and pick up the pieces.

CHAPTER FIVE

Thursday evening couldn't come soon enough for Tess. Her list of questions for Jay grew each day. Alice had scoffed when she'd seen it.

"That's never going to work. Why don't you just let her talk? Start with her brother. Seems to me the sticking point is getting her to talk about Char. How did that relationship work? Everyone at the time knew that Jay Reid was a lesbian. But Char was in the closet. And both had careers that took them out of the country for weeks at a time."

As usual, Alice had nailed it. But Tess wasn't going to let her know that. "Of course," she'd responded. "That's what I was planning to do. These questions are just prompters for me, really."

As she waited for the hours to pass, Tess mulled over the conversation with Donna. She didn't want to hurt her parents, the two women who had lovingly brought her up. But she couldn't ignore the compulsion to find out more about her birth mother. She felt Alice didn't really understand what it meant to her. Had Char cared about giving birth to her at all, or was it just a financial arrangement? She'd carried her for nine months, so there had to be some sort of bond. Tess hoped Jay would be able to give her the answers.

†

Josh texted to say he was going out after work. This happened so rarely that Jay didn't have the heart to tell him he couldn't because of her meeting with Tess. Ritchie could manage without the walk, but he would want his dinner. Making the decision wasn't that hard. She had thought it would be easier to handle Tess's questions in the impersonal surroundings of the clinic. But the girl had already been to the cottage, so what did it matter if she came to the mews?

Mo wasn't in when Jay called her office, but her secretary was able to give her Tess's contact details. She sent her a text with the change of venue, giving her the house number and postcode. Jay was sure Tess would have an app on her phone to help her find it.

When the doorbell chimed, Jay had fed Ritchie and given him a run around the garden. She opened the door to Tess and gave her what she hoped was a welcoming smile before inviting her in. Ritchie greeted the visitor with more enthusiasm than Jay had managed. Maybe he thought she was a new dog walker.

"Ritchie, leave her alone. Would you like a drink? Coffee, tea, wine, beer?"

"I wouldn't mind a glass of wine."

"Right. Red or white?"

"Red, please."

"Well, have a seat. I'll bring it through." As she uncorked a bottle of Malbec, Jay wondered if wine preferences were hereditary. Charley would have chosen red wine as well. She would be amazed at the range of excellent choices available from different countries now.

Jay took the two glasses into the living room and set them on the coffee table. Ritchie had retrieved one of his squeaky toys from his basket and sat gazing up at Tess. But she wasn't paying him any attention; her eyes were riveted on the photographs Jay had placed there earlier.

"That's your dad."

"Yes. I recognise him from the Wimbledon image. Who's the man with him?"

"That's Douglas Rennie. They both worked on Piper Alpha. Dougie was on shore, though, when the explosion happened."

"Was Dougie his boyfriend?"

"Yeah. How did you know that?"

"Easy to see from the way they're smiling in this photo. And my mum, Donna, told me your brother was gay."

"What else did she tell you?"

"Nothing much she could tell me. She'd never met you or your brother. Can you tell me more about him?"

Jay picked up one of the photos. Stewart was grinning from ear to ear holding up his catch. One of his last fly-fishing trips with Dougie…the Kilmartin River on Skye. He had given her the photograph when they met up before her Wimbledon finals match.

"Bit of a cliché, I guess, but he was a gentle giant. Apart from fishing, his other main passion was rugby. He helped his school's under-14 team win all their matches for two years because he was bigger than all the other boys his age."

"Could he have played professionally?"

"Maybe. But he sustained a serious neck injury during his first year at university. Kept him out of the game for over a year. By then he was getting into his studies and starting to look at job opportunities. The North Sea oil fields were an obvious fit with his qualifications, and the 1980s was a good time for the industry."

"Isn't production down now?"

"Yes. It peaked in the mid-eighties and late nineties."

"Does Dougie still work there?"

"He's sixty-one now and thinking of retiring in a few years. After Piper Alpha, he worked only for land-based oil companies. And that's taken him all over the world."

"So, did Char…Charley know your brother? I mean, how did he end up being the sperm donor?"

Jay closed her eyes.

"So, you're going to go through with it?"

Charley stood in what Jay thought of as her Boudicca-chariot-driving stance, swirls of red hair flying around her face. "I need the money, Jay. This research is vital. Thousands of seals are dying and we don't know why."

"Stewie will lend you money. And if I win a few tournaments…."

"I'm not asking your brother for money."

"Not even for your precious seals."

"That's a low blow."

"And what about the pregnancy? That's nine months out of your life."

"Being pregnant doesn't stop the brain working. Or the body. As long as I'm healthy, I can keep working up to the last minute."

"And what about...?"

Charley flew at her then and tackled her onto the couch.

"Sex. Is that all you think about?"

"Yes." With Charley lying on top of her, smothering her with kisses, Jay knew she'd lost the argument, again.

She opened her eyes and looked at the young woman seated opposite. "I introduced them. He was thrilled to be asked."

†

Tess would love to know where Jay went when the faraway look took over her face. She'd seen it before at the cottage. Wherever Jay had gone this time, her face showed conflicting emotions of pain and pleasure. Had there been an argument? She could imagine the twenty-year-old Jay, just starting to make gains in her tennis career, not wanting her lover to have a baby. For someone else. Suggesting her brother as the donor may have helped her to feel included in the process.

Her next question was the one Alice had told her should definitely be taken off the list. But it was out of her mouth before she could stop herself.

"Did they have sex?"

"What? You think it was like some scene out of *The Handmaid's Tale*. Me holding Charley between my legs while my brother pumped his seed into her. OfStewart."

Tess couldn't tell if Jay was angry or not. But then she burst out laughing.

"I'm sorry. I shouldn't have asked that."

Jay gulped some of her wine. "No, you want the details. If you must know, we used a turkey baster. Charley wanted it done properly. Muted lighting in the bedroom, soft music playing in the background."

"Did you feel emotionally involved when she got pregnant?"

"Not really. I was amazed it worked. I'd heard it didn't always take using that method. I didn't see much of her during the pregnancy. She was away at sea for weeks at a time for the first six months. It actually worked out well for her. Just when the bump was getting bigger, she was able to stay home and work on her dissertation. I was travelling quite a bit to overseas tournaments. When we did meet up, we argued a lot. She probably saw more of your parents at that time. Stewart took an interest too. Particularly in the later stages. Whenever he had more than a week off the platform, he would spend time with Charley at the cottage."

Seal View. That moment when she felt she'd been there before. Could a foetus have pre-birth memories of a place? It didn't seem likely, but what other explanation could there be for the feeling that came over her as she stood in the doorway of that low-ceilinged room with the stone fireplace? She could even smell the wood smoke.

Jay poured out more wine for them both. Tess was surprised to see she had emptied her own glass.

"Did my parents, Cheryl and Donna that is, ever visit the cottage?"

"I don't know. They may have done. Why do you ask?"

"I just experienced this vague feeling when I was there. Like déjà vu, you know."

"Well, if they did, I didn't know about it."

Tess wished she could bring out the list she'd prepared. Questions were jumbling around in her head. "I guess one reason I want to know more about my birth parents is the question of hereditary diseases. I don't have a medical history to draw on. Am I at risk from breast cancer, for example?"

"I'm afraid I can't help you with that, either. Charley was an orphan. She grew up in foster care. There may have been records of her parents, but she didn't pursue them. They abandoned her and she wasn't interested in knowing anything about them."

"How could she give up her own baby, then?"

"It was a different situation. You weren't being discarded. She knew you were going to a loving home. At the time she thought that was the best solution. All her time and energy was devoted to saving the seals."

"Is that what you argued about?"

Jay's smile didn't reach her eyes. "Mostly. I was young and stupid. I thought I could make her choose between me or the seals. But what was I thinking? She wasn't going to be happy following me around the tennis circuit. Sitting in hotel rooms in strange cities. She was a brilliant academic. Do you know her doctorate was awarded posthumously?"

"Well, yes. I did read that she'd completed her PhD thesis just before...."

The front door banged shut and the terrier gave a short bark before getting to his feet and going to the top of the stairs. He stood looking down, his tail wagging frantically. Footsteps on the stairs came closer, and the person who appeared moments later stopped all thoughts in Tess's mind.

The person was dressed in black jeans and a tailored black shirt. Apart from the short hair and hint of designer stubble on the cheeks, she could have been seeing herself in the mirror.

"Back early." Jay rose to greet the vision.

"Yeah. It was just one drink."

A look passed between the two that Tess couldn't interpret.

"Um, Josh. This is Tess. We were just going over some family history."

Josh's eyes scanned her briefly before turning to Jay. "Are we related?"

"Yes. You have the same mother."

"I didn't know I had a sister."

"Ditto." Tess didn't have any difficulty reading the panicked look in Jay's eyes this time. "That I had a brother, I mean."

Josh shrugged off his jacket. "I'll just get a beer, and then you can introduce us properly, Mum."

They sat in awkward silence until Josh returned. Jay seemed to find something interesting in the bottom of her wine glass. Tess's gaze roamed around the room. Shelves full of books lined one wall. She would have liked a closer look to see the reading material the two inhabitants favoured.

Josh came back with a bottle in hand and perched on the other end of the sofa. Ritchie had been following him closely and sat by his feet, contented when Josh scratched behind his ears.

"Well, this is a well-kept secret. Where have you been hiding?" His blue gaze met hers.

Jay answered before Tess could open her mouth. "Charley gave her up for adoption."

Josh picked up the foremost photo on the table. "Is Dougie her father as well?"

"No, it was my brother." Jay poured herself another glass of wine.

"Uncle Stewie. Wow."

†

Jay hadn't wanted this to happen, not at this moment in time anyway. Tess's quick remark only reinforced what she'd realised on first meeting the girl. She had Charley's ability to make connections where no one else expected them. Seeing them seated together was unreal. A double vision of Charley.

"Look, Tess. I'm sure you have many more questions, but I'm not really up to answering them tonight. Can we leave it there for now?"

"Yeah. Okay." Tess picked up her bag and coat.

"I'll see you out." Josh leapt to his feet.

When Josh returned a few minutes later, he gave Jay a quick kiss on the cheek. "The night's still young. I'm off to the The Churchill. Do you want to come?"

"No, thanks. I am really quite bushed."

"Right, see you in a bit. No, Ritchie. Stay."

Jay heard the door slam as he left. No surprise, really. She was sure he was going to meet up with Tess at the pub. Nothing she could do to stop it. The time had come, as she knew it would one day. The time to stop hiding.

She drank the last of the wine and sat back in the recliner, pulling the lever to raise the footrest. The effects of the drink mixed with the strain of the last hour, and she was almost asleep when the doorbell rang.

†

Deuce

Amanda couldn't bear the sight of the drooping roses any longer. She pitched them headfirst into the bin and took the vase to the sink in the kitchen next to the office. Jay hadn't come back to her place the previous night, claiming to be tired and having paperwork to finish. It sounded like a feeble excuse. As far as she knew, Mo Farrell looked after Jay's business accounts. Amanda desperately wanted to talk to Jay about Charlotte Summersbridge.

During one of her coffee breaks during the day, she'd trawled the Internet for information and found several articles. One of them had a clear head-and-shoulders photo. Attractive possibly, if you liked the red-haired, blue-eyed combination. Only a few days short of her thirtieth birthday when the boat went down; the articles gave nothing away about Charlotte's private life, mainly quoting from her work on the dying seal population.

Jay still hadn't phoned or texted by the time Amanda got home. She discarded her work clothes and stood inside her walk-in closet pondering what to wear. On nights without her lover's distracting presence, she would lounge in front of the telly with a takeaway, comfortable in her well-worn tracksuit.

Was Jay at home? A lot of the excuses for not seeing Amanda revolved around Josh. He was twenty-four. Surely he didn't want his mother hanging around all the time.

She'd only been to the mews house once before. And that was only because Josh was away somewhere. This was ridiculous. She was Jay's fiancée. She should be able to see her anytime she wanted.

Mind made up, Amanda selected a blouse she knew Jay liked and a tight-fitting short skirt. The choice of underwear was easy. She had a drawer full of skimpy items, continually replenished as Jay more often than not ripped them off her body in her haste to make love to her. She often played rough and Amanda enjoyed it, revelling in the fiery passion Jay ignited.

Although she had been to the house before, the location was a hazy memory, as Jay was holding her hand and she was anticipating how they would spend the next few hours. Amanda walked up and down a few streets in the general vicinity before she saw the archway leading to the mews. The cobbled stones underfoot made walking in high heels a hazardous affair. Something else she'd forgotten from the previous visit.

Lights were on in the upstairs window that she thought was the kitchen. If she remembered rightly, the living room faced the enclosed garden at the back, floor-to-ceiling windows letting in more light than she'd expected in the compact dwelling. Jay had proudly informed her that Josh's architectural enhancements were responsible for the modern look of the inside of the house.

Josh again. He was obviously the main rival for Jay's affections. Why couldn't he have got a job in another city? Amanda took a deep breath, steeling herself to walk across and ring the doorbell.

She hadn't taken a step when the door opened. A young woman came out, smiling as she adjusted her shoulder bag. In the light from the one ancient streetlamp lighting the mews, Amanda could see her face clearly. She didn't realise she was holding her breath until the woman had passed through the archway on to the main road. The likeness was unmistakable. Charlotte Summersbridge as she had looked in the old newspaper photograph.

Deuce

The door opened again and Josh came out. He didn't look around, just huddled into his thin jacket and walked quickly through the arch. Just Jay and the dog in the house now. Part of her mind told her to go back to her flat and numb her thoughts with a bottle of tequila for company. The other part told her to go in and get some answers. Jay had a lot of explaining to do.

CHAPTER SIX

Tess found the pub easily from Josh's whispered directions when he'd escorted her downstairs to the door. It wasn't too busy. The commuter crowd would all have gone by now, having whiled away an hour or two after work to miss the worst of the evening crush on the tube.

She ordered a lime and soda for herself and a pint of beer for Josh. After the two glasses of wine Jay had given her, she wanted to keep a clear head for this conversation.

Josh arrived at the same time as the bartender finished pulling the pint. "I'll get these." He took a tenner out of his pocket and handed it over before she could protest. "There's a free table near the fireplace. Have a seat and I'll bring the drinks over."

Tess complied, thinking he'd certainly mastered the art of chivalry, placing her bag between her feet as she sat. For a moment, she thought about getting her phone out to record their chat. But she reminded herself that this was a personal quest, not a journalistic one.

"So, what did Mum tell you about Charley?" he asked as soon as he sat opposite.

"You call Jay Mum, even though she isn't your mother."

"I was still a baby when Charley died. Jay's the only mother I've known."

"And Douglas Rennie's your father?"

"Yeah. But I call him Dougie. He's not really done the dad thing. I mean, he and Jay are friends but not partners."

"I get that. I know she's a lesbian. Does she have a current girlfriend?"

Josh put his glass back down on the table and swiped at his mouth with the back of his hand in a self-conscious gesture. "Yes, but I'm not going to gossip about my mum."

"Okay." Tess took a sip of her own drink before asking, "So when did you transition?"

"Wow. We've only just met. How did you know?"

"Just a sort of look. A girl in my Year 11 class went through it. But that was like fifteen years ago. She found it really hard to be accepted. At the end of the year she—sorry, he—went to a different school to do sixth form. How was it for you?"

"Fifteen years ago I was nine. Up to that time I was fairly happy being a tomboy. Jay never tried to make me wear dresses or do normal girl-type things. But, you know, it was always there from an early age. I just knew I was meant to be a boy. I would dream that one day I would wake up as a boy."

"When did you...I'm not sure how to word this...you know, figure out it wasn't going to happen magically overnight?"

"About the time I stopped believing in Santa Claus and the Tooth Fairy." Josh studied her over the rim of his glass. "Anyway, where have you been hiding all these years? How come I didn't know anything about you until tonight?"

"I didn't know until recently that neither of my mothers, the two women who brought me up, were actually my birth mother. None of their eggs were involved. I only vaguely remembered a woman I called Auntie Char who occasionally turned up with a belated birthday or Christmas present. And then she disappeared from our lives."

"You have more memories of her than I do. Jay's kept all her things that she left in the cottage. In the attic."

"What kind of things?"

"Clothes, books, research notes, and lots of photos. Jay even kept all her music albums even though we don't have a record player. I sometimes sit up there looking at the pictures of Jay and Charley, Uncle Stewie and Dougie. They look so happy. I can't help thinking about what it would have been like if Stewie and Charley were still alive. How different would our lives have been? Jay does her best to hide it from me, but I know she thinks about them all the time."

Tess sipped her drink and wondered how she could get access to the attic. Her journalistic senses were kicking in. Befriending Josh was a step in that direction. He seemed keen to embrace her as his long-lost sister. Although she'd told Jay she didn't want to drive out to the Norfolk coast again, it would be worth it to get a peek at the remnants of Char's life.

†

Amanda pressed the doorbell and waited. Unlike in her apartment building, the small house had no entry phone. Of course, really Jay should have given her a key. Just another example of how little she let Amanda into her life. She heard the dog barking. What was its name? She didn't really like dogs. When they were married, the dog would have to live with Josh.

Jay opened the door looking flushed. It couldn't have been from running down the stairs. "Oh, hi. What are you doing here?"

Not exactly the enthusiastic greeting she hoped for from her fiancée. "We need to talk. That girl who just left looked remarkably like Charlotte Summersbridge. Don't you think it's time you told me about her?"

"Come in." Jay walked away from the door.

The dog looked up at her briefly, then turned and followed Jay. Amanda closed the door and joined the procession.

Evidence of Jay's previous visitor cluttered the coffee table in the living room. Two wine glasses, and a beer bottle hardly touched. The wine glasses were empty and so was the bottle of what looked like an expensive Malbec. That could explain the flush on Jay's cheeks.

"Do you want a drink?"

"I wouldn't mind a glass of white if you've got any chilled."

Jay disappeared around the corner to the kitchen area. Amanda sat on the sofa, and the dog jumped up beside her. She tried to fend off his advances as he moved onto her lap and attempted to lick her face.

"Ritchie, get down."

The dog obeyed and sat on the floor. Jay placed a glass of white wine in front of Amanda. In her other hand she held a glass of water.

"Sorry about that." She sat in the chair opposite and called the dog over, inviting him to sit on her lap. He settled down after she'd petted him and let him lick her face.

She'll need to wash that off before she gets another kiss from me. Amanda sipped her wine. It was well chilled.

"What do you want to know? It seems all I've done this evening is talk about Charley."

Charley, was it? Lynne was right. There was a personal connection, a very personal one.

"Well, she obviously means a lot to you. I mean, I know she's dead and has been for a long time. But you named your clinic after her."

"Yes, she was my lover. More than that. My soul mate. She gave birth to Josh and we were going to bring him up together. The start of our family."

Each word from Jay's mouth was a stab in the heart. "Lover" she had expected. But not "soul mate", "family".

"What about the other one?"

Jay sipped her water, absentmindedly stroking the dog's ears. Amanda felt a twinge of jealousy. Wouldn't she love that hand stroking her? It would need washing first, though.

"Oh. You mean Tess. Charley had her while she was at uni and gave her up for adoption to a lesbian couple who wanted a child but neither of the women was able to carry one."

"Has this Tess always been part of your life?"

"No. We only met the weekend before last. She's a journalist and obtained an interview through Mo saying she wanted to write a book about my tennis career. But then she discovered that Charley was her birth mother, and since then she has been on a mission to find out more about her."

"How long were you with…Charley?"

Deuce

"Seven years as lovers, but we knew each other a few years before."

"How did you meet?"

"My parents wanted me to go to university. I wasn't keen. All I really wanted to do was play tennis. Anyway, I got an interview at Exeter University. Charley was a second-year student there and was assigned to show me around."

"You were going to study marine biology?"

"No, of course not. The physical-education degree came under the same department, though. It's called something different now. Health science or something like that. I didn't get past the first two terms. As I've told you before, my parents were killed in a car crash. Stewart initially thought I should carry on and get the degree as they'd wished. But my thinking was that if their lives could end so suddenly, so could mine. I knew sitting in a classroom wasn't the way I wanted to spend the next few years. He didn't take much persuading to let me follow my dream of becoming a tennis pro."

"Did your relationship with Charley start while you were at uni?"

"I don't know why this is important to you. It was a long time ago."

"It's obviously still important to you. That's why I want to know. We're going to be married in just over a week. We shouldn't have any secrets."

Jay looked drained and Amanda knew she was pushing it. But she wanted answers.

†

Jay closed her eyes. She wished Amanda would stop asking questions. That first time with Charley wasn't something she could share with her. A summer tournament and her first win as a professional. Not the whole tournament, but the match that got her into the semi-final. She hadn't even known that Charley was there while she was playing. Probably a good thing, she'd thought afterwards. Her concentration would have been shot.

The attraction had been there from the day they met. While Charley took her round the university campus, Jay had barely been able to concentrate. She couldn't imagine that this gorgeous woman would be remotely interested in her. Their first date happened more or less by accident at the end of Michaelmas term just before the start of Christmas break. Not really a date. They had both been at the same end-of-term dance organised by the student union. Jay only decided to go at the last minute.

Charley was popular with the boys. Never without a dance partner, but she didn't seem to have a boyfriend claiming her attention. During a break in the music, Jay finally plucked up the courage to talk to her. She didn't dance with her then but agreed to meet her for coffee the next day.

All through the spring term, they danced around each other. Jay loved spending time with Charley, but it was getting harder to be with her and not be any closer than the friendship Charley offered. The day that changed was a day of firsts and the start of the rollercoaster ride that ended so abruptly seven years later.

Jay opened the bedroom door and stepped inside, dropping her tennis kit by the closet. Stewart hadn't been able to get time off to come to the tournament, but he'd booked her in to the best hotel in the town.

Charley gasped as she moved past Jay to take in the four-poster double bed, the seating area in front of the window, and door leading on to a balcony.

"I know you won today. But you still can't afford this."

"No. Stewie can, though. And he's stumped up for this as well." Jay read the card on the tray holding the ice bucked with a full-size bottle of champagne nestled inside. "'To the next British number one. You were ace today, Baby Bird.'"

"Hm, Baby Bird, is it?" Charley's eyes twinkled mischievously.

"Don't you start. He only gets away with it because he's bigger than me."

Charley stood on tiptoe so their noses touched. "Think you can handle me, Baby Bird?"

Jay grabbed her shoulders and kissed her mouth, relishing the soft feel of the lips she'd wanted to savour from the first moment she'd seen Charley on campus. After a few heavenly moments, she broke the connection and pulled back to study the face inches from her own.

"Are you sure about this?" Jay's gaze locked on to the mesmerising blue eyes.

"Never been surer."

"Champagne now?"

"Maybe later."

Jay couldn't recall afterwards which one of them made the first move. She had thought she would be able to play it cool, not wanting to let her inexperience show. Charley had never mentioned having any previous lovers. All these months she'd deflected any conversation veering on to the topic. But it was Charley who took charge.

"You were so beautiful out there on court. I can't believe everyone watching wasn't as turned on as I was."

"You're making me blush." Lying naked next to the woman she'd dreamt of for months, Jay was already consumed by heat.

"Impossible." Charley moved slowly, sensually down Jay's body, caressing her gently with her hands and her lips until she reached her goal. Jay's arousal had already reached a peak by the time Charley's mouth settled on the wet opening awaiting her attention. Jay lost control of her hips, arching as each stroke of Charley's tongue increased the intensity of the orgasm building inside.

When Charley added first one finger, then two, and a third, Jay thought she would lose her mind.

Gasping as the tidal wave of the climax subsided, she was overcome with emotions she didn't know existed until then.

Charley pulled herself up and kissed her, juices dripping down her chin. Jay welcomed the taste of herself, letting their tongues dance together. As Charley broke the kiss to catch her breath, her eyes bored into Jay's, the depths of blue capturing her as they always did. "How was it? An ace?"

"Better. Two in a row at least."

From that first time to the last, the intensity of their lovemaking never lessened.

"Can I stay tonight?"

"I'm sorry, Amanda. I really don't have any energy." Jay knew she couldn't make love to her with thoughts of Charley swirling around.

Ritchie sat up and jumped off the chair just as Josh appeared in the doorway. "Hi, Amanda."

"Oh, hi, Josh. I'll be off, then. See you tomorrow?"

"I'm not sure. We have the final suit fitting, don't we, Josh?"

"Yeah. They look great, Amanda." He was shifting from foot to foot, a mannerism Jay knew well. "Uh, could we have a chat, Mum?"

"Of course." She got to her feet slowly. "Can you see yourself out, Amanda?"

"I'll come down with you. I think Ritchie needs a toilet break." Josh led the way, and after a searing glance at Jay, Amanda followed.

Jay drank another glass of water while waiting for Josh to return from giving Ritchie a run around the garden. Once they were all three settled in the living room again, she waited for Josh to speak. He was picking at imaginary lint on his trousers.

"Spit it out, son. I'm not getting any younger."

"I met up with Tess in the pub."

"Yes, I thought that's what you were doing."

"You're not mad."

"No. It's only natural you would be curious about her."

"The thing is, though, how did she know, as soon as she saw me? Most people don't."

Jay didn't need to ask what he meant. But this question hadn't surfaced for several years now. "Well, she's been researching her background and has probably studied any photos of Charley she could find. It may be your nose. Or lack of an Adam's apple."

"But it was like she instantly knew."

"Maybe just intuition, a sibling thing."

Josh touched his nose. "Do you think I should have a nose job?"

"Not unless you really feel unhappy about it. Personally, I don't think it's a problem. And you have a bigger operation to consider."

Josh nodded and looked at his feet. They'd talked it over many times, but Jay knew he was still undecided on taking the final step. The stages he'd already passed through had made him extremely happy. His body had reacted well to the hormone treatments through his teens and the double mastectomy she'd bought him for his twenty-first birthday.

"Amanda didn't seem very happy," he offered, finding his voice again.

"Oh."

"She asked me if I thought you really loved her."

"What did you say?"

"I said you wouldn't be marrying her if you didn't."

Jay sighed. She did feel drained from all the talk about Charley. And now this. Sleep wasn't going to come easily.

Chapter Seven

"So how did it go? Did she talk to you about Charlotte?" Lynne couldn't stop herself from asking as soon as they met outside the bridal boutique on Saturday morning.

"Yes. More than I wanted to know. And it wasn't so much what she said as the look on her face when she mentioned her name. Charley. If the woman weren't already dead, I'd want to kill her."

"What about the mystery weekends?"

"I didn't get a chance to ask. Josh came in and she clammed up. And with him there, I couldn't stay the night. Honestly. Talk about children being weaned, I think she's the one who won't let go of him."

Lynne followed her into the shop. They were ten minutes early for the appointment, but the dressmaker was ready for them. Amanda disappeared through a doorway, and Lynne sat in one of the chairs by the window. She flicked through the bridal magazines, wondering at all the different dresses and accessories displayed. Amanda had been secretive about her choice. Lynne hoped she hadn't gone over the top. Somehow she didn't think Jay Reid was the type to go in for all the big-wedding hype.

When Amanda emerged from the fitting room, Lynne gasped. The simple white sheath dress emphasised all her friend's curves. "You look stunning. I'd certainly marry you." She cringed inwardly. A stupid thing to say but luckily Amanda was too absorbed in twirling around in front of the mirror to check out the dress from all angles.

"Do you think Jay will like it?"

"I'm sure she will. No doubt about it."

Amanda was practically skipping down the street when they left the boutique. "I can't wait. This time next week we'll be married."

Lynne kept pace with her and tried to shake off the feeling that the fairy-tale ending Amanda envisioned would only end in tears. Viewing their relationship from the outside, solely from Amanda's point of view, the sex was great but they shared little else. Amanda had done all the running. She had even proposed to Jay. The mystery Lynne grappled with was why Jay Reid said yes. Seeing her lover two or three nights a week was all she'd offered of herself. A week before the wedding and Amanda still didn't know where Jay spent her weekends.

Maybe there was no other physical woman in the picture, but the ghostly presence of Charlotte Summersbridge was all too real.

†

Mo parked outside the cottage and pulled her helmet off. A freshening breeze blew through her hair. Even if she didn't need to see Jay, she enjoyed the ride to the coast. It was good to get out of the city and she didn't do it often enough these days.

Ritchie ran up to greet her as soon as she rounded the corner of the cottage. Jay followed more sedately, looking windblown from a trek to the beach.

"Hey, wasn't expecting you today."

"No. Could have waited until Monday, but I fancied the ride. Papers for you to sign."

"Okay. Good timing. Coffee or something stronger?"

"Coffee. You look like you could do with a caffeine boost."

"Is that your way of saying I look like shit?"

"Yes."

"Thanks. I haven't slept much the last two nights." Jay led the way into the house.

Mo sat at the kitchen table and took the file out of her backpack while Jay moved around setting up the coffee maker and taking two mugs out of a cupboard. She seated herself opposite while they waited for the machine to filter the water through the grounds.

"So what's keeping you awake?"

"A lot of things got stirred up this week. Tess came to see me, wanting to know about her biological parents. Josh arrived home while we were talking, so they are now comparing notes as siblings. He was upset at first because Tess immediately sussed him as trans. And on the same evening, Amanda turned up with questions about Charley."

The coffee maker burbled to its conclusion and Jay got up to pour the coffee. When she sat down again, she faced

Mo with an anguished expression. "I can't marry Amanda. I don't love her."

Mo stirred milk into her coffee and tried to keep the sarcasm out of her voice. "That's stating the bleeding obvious." Relenting, she reached across and grasped Jay's arm. "Have you told her yet?"

"No. How do you go about dumping your fiancée a week before the wedding? I'm not on Facebook. Text maybe?"

"I know you're not serious. If you can't face her in person, at least do it by phone." Mo placed her other hand on the file she'd brought. "Do you still want to go ahead with signing the mews house over to Josh?"

"Yes. Absolutely. I need to secure his future."

"And what are you going to do? Hide out here again?"

"No. I'll keep working. If and when Josh wants me to move out I'll find somewhere to rent."

"Josh isn't likely to kick you out, is he?"

"Not at the moment. But he won't want me hanging around when he gets a steady girlfriend."

"Does he know you're doing this?" Mo opened the file.

"No. It's a surprise. An early twenty-fifth-birthday present."

"Lucky boy."

"Man." Jay smiled for the first time since Mo's arrival. "He was so thrilled with the suit when we went for the final fitting yesterday." Her smile disappeared. "I didn't have the heart to tell him he might not get to wear it for the wedding."

Mo flipped to the page at the back of the document and handed Jay a pen. She watched her sign where she'd put small crosses. Her signature as witness was already there. She returned the file to her backpack and waited for Jay to finish pouring another coffee for both of them. "Call her now."

Jay stared into her mug and let out a huge sigh.

"I know you. You'll keep putting it off and before you know it, you'll be walking up that aisle and saying, 'I do', even though you don't mean it." Mo glanced around the kitchen and spotted Jay's phone on the counter by the fridge.

†

"How about a coffee?" Lynne asked as they passed Starbucks, still trying to keep up with Amanda's energised pace.

"Oh no. I can't. The dress fits perfectly now."

"Have a glass of water, then. I'm gasping."

Amanda slowed and looked at her. "Okay. I'd really like a celebratory drink. But that's out of the question until after the wedding."

She let Lynne steer her into the café and over to a table with comfy seats by the window. It had been recently vacated by the looks of the empty cups and plates that hadn't been cleared. Amanda sat while Lynne located a tray and took away all the debris. A parade of elephants could have passed by on the street and she wouldn't have noticed. Her mind's eye was seeing her walking down the aisle in that white dress, Jay waiting for her looking impossibly handsome.

Lynne returned with a glass of water and a large cappuccino before the vows were exchanged. Amanda smiled at her, still partly in her dream world. "Thanks for coming with me today."

"Well, I've never been a bridesmaid before, but I figured it was part of my duties."

Her phone's ringtone sounded before she could reply. Amanda fumbled in her bag and smiled broadly when she saw the name on the screen. "It's Jay." She accepted the call and held the phone to her ear. "Hello, sweetheart. I've just been trying on my dress. It's fabulous."

"I'm sure it is. I'm sorry, Amanda. But I can't go through with it."

"What do you mean?" The words didn't register right away.

"I mean I can't marry you."

"Why? Why not? What's wrong?" Amanda could feel the tears gathering.

"We are. Or I am, anyway. I don't know how to say this without hurting you. But the truth is, I'm not in love with you."

"Is there someone else?" The tears fell rapidly now and she couldn't keep the tremor from her voice.

"No."

"It's her, isn't it?" Stirrings of anger coursed through her body. "That woman from your past. She's dead, Jay."

"I'm sorry." Jay ended the call.

Amanda stared at the screen and gulped back her tears. She accepted the napkin Lynne handed her and wiped her face. "I guess you heard that."

"Yes. Not unexpected, I'm afraid."

"Well I didn't see it coming."

"Come on, Amanda. She's hardly a candidate for Lover of the Year. Someone who disappears every weekend without explanation. I would have called her on that the first time it happened. You've been engaged for six months."

"What am I going to do? All the preparations, the venue, the catering, the honeymoon...."

Lynne placed a hand on hers. "That can be taken care of. If you call today, I'm sure the venue and the food can be cancelled without incurring a fee. As for the honeymoon, I've always wanted to visit Corsica."

†

Jay placed the phone on the table and frowned at Mo. "There wasn't any other way, was there?"

"A bit brutal. But no, I guess not. You could have saved her the heartache by not agreeing to marry her in the first place."

"I know. I regretted it the moment I said yes."

"But you let all the preparations go ahead? What were you thinking?"

"I guess I wasn't. I sort of got caught up with the idea of being married."

"Well, in a way she's right, you know."

"About what?"

"About Charley. You've never let her go."

There wasn't anything she could say to that. It was true. Every time she thought she could attempt to put the reality of Charley's death behind her, memories of their time together would charge through her dreams and continue to surface when she woke. Jay knew it was wishful thinking, but part of her couldn't believe that Charley was really dead. Remembering her as a living, breathing person kept her going. Kept her from walking into the sea to join her.

Mo finished her coffee and stood. "Better be off. Where's Josh today?"

"Visiting friends in Brighton."

"So just you and Ritchie." Mo reached down to pat the terrier, who had come into the kitchen as soon as she moved. "You take care of your mum."

His tail wagged as if he understood, but Jay knew he was just hoping she was moving towards his biscuit tin. Jay got up and hugged Mo. "Thanks…for everything."

"Yeah, sure. I'm adding relationship guidance counsellor to my list of services." Mo held on briefly, then moved away. "Call me when you get back in to town. Tuesday evening, lasagna and garlic bread."

"Sounds good. Count me in."

With the sounds of Mo's bike growing fainter, Jay shook herself. There were people she needed to tell about the wedding cancellation. It wasn't a big list. Josh, Dougie, staff from the clinic. They could all wait until Monday. Except Dougie. If he'd only planned to visit London because of the wedding, he might need advance notice to make other arrangements so he could make the most of his time off before setting out for another oil field thousands of miles away.

He answered on the first ring. "What's up, Jay Bird?"

She let him get away with that greeting. It was a compromise, after she'd threatened to kneecap him when he tried calling her Baby Bird. Stewie's nickname for her didn't sit right coming from anyone else.

"The wedding's off."

"Oh, what's happened?"

"I just came to my senses. Realised I couldn't go through with it."

"Too bad. You'll miss out on seeing me in a penguin suit."

"You weren't…."

"Well, you'll never know now. But, seriously, are you okay?"

"Yeah. I should have done it before. Amanda deserves better. My heart was never really in it."

"Right. I'm going to be in London anyway at the end of the week. So let's meet up."

Jay agreed, and when he ended the call, she felt better. Ritchie pawed at her leg. She understood the signal and reached into his biscuit tin to hand him a treat. While he munched, she decided to take a run up to the seal sanctuary. Watching the large sea mammals always had a soothing effect on her.

†

Tess rolled over into the space Alice had recently vacated. A Saturday shift meant she was on her own for the day. Their regular lunch with the parents was off too. But instead of the free day she would have relished, she was meeting Donna in town. Cheryl was at a reunion with her old university pals in York, and they were taking advantage of her absence to finalise plans for her sixty-fifth birthday. A surprise party. Tess didn't think a surprise was a good idea for someone that age. Could give her a heart attack.

Pulling the duvet close around her body, she revelled in the warmth, and drifted off to sleep. When she woke again, the room was lighter than it had been before. She rubbed her eyes and edged over to Alice's side of the bed. The digital figures glared at her showing 9:47. Damn, she barely had time to get dressed to be on time. Donna would be pacing Selfridges Foodhall like a feral tiger if she weren't there at 10:30 on the dot.

Setting the all-time record for washing, dressing, and leaving the house without forgetting anything vital...keys, money, phone, Oyster card...Tess reached her destination only ten minutes late. She found Donna inspecting the boxed-chocolate selections.

"Morning, love." Donna kissed her cheek and turned back to the display. "What do you think? I'm tempted by this one." She indicated a box with drawers, each containing a selection of mouthwatering chocolates. "It's different, isn't it?"

Tess looked at it. "Hm. I don't know. I like that one better." She pointed to a smaller box with the chocolates built up in a pyramid. "Depends how much you want to spend, though. That other one is way more expensive."

"You know how much Cheryl loves her chocolates. And she's only sixty-five once."

"Why didn't you just order online? Either of these is going to be awkward to carry home."

"I couldn't risk her opening whatever was delivered."

"Well, send it to me, then. I can arrange to be in."

"Oh, would you, sweetie? That's a great idea. I was wondering where I would be able to hide it."

While Donna paid and made the delivery arrangements, Tess wandered around, awed by the selection of so much fine food and drink that she couldn't afford.

There were a few more stops along Oxford Street to gather other items for the party. It was a fine day, so they wandered down Regent Street, looking in windows and generally behaving like tourists.

"Fortnum's for lunch?" Donna asked when they reached Piccadilly Circus.

Tess would have preferred a pub or a wine bar, but this was Donna's day out, so she agreed half-heartedly. Expecting to be sitting in front of a pot of tea and selection of gourmet sandwiches, Tess was delighted when Donna led the way to the downstairs wine bar. She'd forgotten it was there.

Donna grinned at her once they were seated. "My treat. For dragging you around the shops."

"Thank you." Tess felt a pang of guilt. Donna wasn't going to be happy with her continued pursuit of information about her birth parents. Or the discovery of a half-sibling. She decided to wait until they'd enjoyed their meal and a few glasses of wine before confessing.

Over lunch they covered general topics: her job, Alice's, Donna's involvement in golf-club politics.

"That's something you could do a piece on, love. Exploring why, in this day and age, golf clubs still get away with marginalising women."

"You'd have to write it. I don't know enough about golf. Except that it looks mind-numbingly boring."

"You wouldn't say that if you played."

This was an old argument, going nowhere. Tess decided it was time to jump in with both feet. "I saw Jay Reid again this week. Went round to her house, and she showed me photos of Char and Stewart."

Donna's eyes clouded over.

Tess reached across the table and grasped her hand. "Mum, I still love you. And Cheryl. I'm just curious about where I came from."

"You always were a curious child. Forever asking questions we couldn't answer." Donna managed a sad smile. "No surprise you became a journalist."

"I also found out I have a half-sibling. Char gave birth to another child not long before she disappeared. That's why she stopped coming to see us and it's the real reason Jay gave up playing tennis. She had a baby to look after."

"Really. That didn't make it into the news at the time."

"That's not all that didn't get reported. I haven't been able to find much at all about Char's research vessel sinking. It's like there was some sort of news blackout surrounding it. Like it disappeared into a black hole."

"I know how your mind works. Are you thinking there was a government cover-up?"

"I can't think why. She was researching this virus that was decimating seal colonies, not tracking nuclear submarines."

"Seals. Yes, I remember she was obsessed with their welfare. That stuffed toy she gave you when you were two. You dragged it everywhere until it fell apart. You called it Teddy but it was a sea lion."

"I don't remember that. I've still got the coral necklace she gave me, although it doesn't fit around my neck now." Tess noted that Donna looked happier talking about the past. She decided to leave telling her about meeting with Josh for another time.

Deuce

PART TWO

Chapter Eight

I am Charlotte Summersbridge. Repeating this in my head helps to keep returning memories from crowding in too quickly. I need to stem the flow or be overwhelmed. As I stare out the small window as the plane flies lower over the city, London looks familiar, yet different. But I suppose everything will. Even Jay.

The last few weeks have passed in a whirlwind. From seeing the seal on the sand, to Konrad's panicked fear that his mother has gone mad, to trying to convince officials I am someone other than the person all my friends and neighbours thought I was.

Katrin Nielsen didn't register on any Faroe Islands records. I have no status. The officials were eventually persuaded my story had merit when they saw the images picked up from the Internet. They conceded I resemble the young marine biologist who met with an untimely death. But

Deuce

how had I ended up on the east coast of Suðuroy? It was much further north than the last known location of the research vessel.

Like putting together a jigsaw puzzle, there are missing pieces, some bits I can join up, while others remain scattered across the table. I know there had been a storm, equipment was damaged, and we were blown off course.

A team of divers was sent to look for the wreck, mainly to convince the authorities that I wasn't some madwoman. That they found it, half a mile offshore from the village I stumbled into, was another shock to my recovering memories. I had looked over that stretch of sea every day for the last twenty-three years.

Now I am travelling to London with Danish embassy officials on a hastily arranged diplomatic passport with the name I was given when I washed up on that remote beach: Katrin Nielsen. They want to keep my other identity secret until the DNA results of all the skeletal remains found with the wreck have been confirmed and relatives informed. My own DNA I have told them can be verified by one of the two children I gave birth to in England.

Konrad wanted to come with me. Excited, once he recovered from the shock of finding out I was someone else, he wants to meet his newly discovered siblings. He has never been off the island, and a trip to London was like flying to the moon in his mind. He was disappointed to be left with a family connected to the Faroese Representation Office in Copenhagen, but I told him there was a lot to sort out, boring details, meetings, and documentation. I also told him he could use his time while I was away to practice speaking English. I'm sure he will be well looked after.

My own excitement mounts as the plane's wheels touch down on the tarmac. But it is mixed with fear too. I can say, "I am Charlotte Summersbridge," but will anyone remember or care?

†

Jay studied the board in the lobby listing all the companies housed in the office building. Bradford Bowen Associates was second from the top on the tenth floor. The lift opened onto a standard reception area. The ficus, situated between two uncomfortable-looking chairs, was covered in dust. The receptionist glanced away from her screen to assess the visitor and tapped a key before speaking. Jay suspected she was playing a game.

"Can I help you?"

"I'd like to see Amanda Bowen."

"Um, she doesn't work here."

"Oh." Jay looked at the picture on the wall behind the reception desk. A skyline punctuated by high-rise buildings. Dubai, she guessed. "Is her father in?"

"Yes. But if you don't have an appointment...."

"Tell him Jay Reid is here. I think he'll want to see me."

She lifted the phone, her expression indicating she thought it a waste of her precious time. Jay enjoyed the change in her attitude when it became clear the great man would indeed see her now.

Buzzed through to the inner sanctum, she walked along to the office at the end of the corridor. The name on the door read: Bradford Bowen, CEO.

She knocked lightly before entering. The grimness of the outer office wasn't replicated here. No expense had been spared on the furniture or decor. The room was dominated, though, by the view through the floor-to-ceiling window. The man behind the wide expanse of a polished wooden desk didn't stand to greet her. Not that she'd expected him to from their previous brief encounter in the restaurant.

"You've got some balls, I'll admit." His tone conveyed more amusement than the anger she'd expected.

"Where's Amanda? I went to her apartment first."

"She's gone to Barcelona. Her professor friend is speaking at a conference there. I guess she wanted to get away for a few days."

"I thought she worked here."

A humourless smile creased Bowen's face. "My daughter is a fantasist. As you would have found out eventually. She works in the admin department of the University of East London. I believe her friend, Dr Lynne Croft, helped her get the job."

"Not a high-flying hedge-fund manager, then?"

"She wouldn't know a hedge fund from a horse's behind."

Jay walked over to the window and gazed across the urban landscape. Traffic and people scurried about on the road far below. "What happened to the flowers I sent?"

"Redirected to either the university or her apartment."

Jay reached into her pocket. She placed the items on the edge of the desk. "The rings and the keycard to her flat. Have the wedding arrangements been cancelled?"

"Yup."

"Any cancellation fees? I'm happy to pay my share."

"No problem. Turns out the venue was double-booked and the caterers hadn't started on the food."

"What about the honeymoon?"

"All sorted. After Barcelona, Amanda and the good professor are going on to Corsica. So you're off the hook on all counts." He stood then and Jay saw he was taller than she'd thought. Long legs and a short torso. She also noted the wince as he held on to the desk while getting to his feet.

"Back pain?"

"What?"

"I'm a physio. I can see you have some discomfort."

"Are you a miracle worker? My doc says I just have to put up with it and it'll wear off eventually. Keep taking the painkillers, he said."

"How long have you had it?"

"Two months."

"That's a long time to be in pain, and to be on the pills. I may be able to help." She fished a card out of her jacket pocket.

He looked at it and raised an eyebrow. "What the fuck is CST when it's at home?"

"Cranial sacral therapy. It's a gentle form of massage and can be effective in relieving some forms of spinal discomfort."

"Are you some kind of quack?"

"No. It is a recognised treatment. I'm also a fully qualified physiotherapist." She backed towards the door. "Think about it. I can't relieve the pain I've caused your daughter, but I might be able to help you."

†

Lynne looked down at her sleeping friend and hoped she would feel better when she woke up. Amanda had consumed four gin and tonics on the two-hour flight from London and immediately crashed out as soon as they got into the hotel room. She'd already pre-loaded at the airport too. Lynne was just glad she had been able to get her on and off the plane without causing a scene. Airlines were less tolerant of drunken passengers these days.

She showered and changed into a lighter outfit—shorts and a long-sleeved T-shirt. Lynne then emptied the contents of her handbag into the room safe and stuffed some euros in one pocket and her phone in the other. Leaving a note for Amanda, she ventured out to explore the hotel and surrounding area. Barcelona was a city she had always wanted to visit, and as she would be ensconced in conference talks for the next few days, she planned to make the most of her free time.

After listening to Amanda's rants about what a selfish shit Jay Reid was for most of the journey, it was a relief to have a few hours to herself. Lynne had tried to give her some perspective, telling her it was better not to have committed to a loveless marriage. Amanda seemed to be under the impression that lesbian marriages were perfect.

†

The rest of the day was filled with client treatments. Jay broke the news of the cancelled wedding to staff during their shared lunch break. Some expressed concern, but Jay assured them it had been her decision and she was happier for it.

Ross knocked on her door shortly after she'd returned to her office.

"Come in."

He stood awkwardly in front of her desk. "Are you really okay with this, boss?"

"Yes, I am. I'm just sorry I left it this long to realise it wasn't what I wanted." Jay gave him a reassuring smile. He was the only staff member who had met Amanda on the few occasions she'd arrived at the clinic to meet Jay for an after-work dinner date.

"How did Amanda take it?"

"Devastated, no doubt. I saw her father this morning and he said she's gone to Barcelona for the week with her best friend. Sounds like they're going to continue on to the honeymoon destination."

"Oh." After a moment's silence, he added, "I'm glad she's not on her own, then."

After he left, Jay shook her head. Ross was a caring soul. That was reflected by the number of clients who returned for therapy sessions with him long after they needed to.

She turned her attention to reading the notes on her next appointment. Keeping busy was the best way to deflect her mind from the conversation she would be having with Josh later. Telling him face-to-face was the only option.

CHAPTER NINE

Jay removed her hands from under the client's lower back and moved quietly around to take up a position behind his head. She hadn't expected to hear from Bradford Bowen again, so she was surprised when the booking appeared on her appointments calendar for Friday morning.

He appeared to be asleep, but she could tell from his breathing that he wasn't. However, he had relaxed into the session much more quickly than she'd thought he would. Some people liked to chat while she worked, but he had stayed silent. It didn't matter to her either way. Talking helped some clients relax.

She held her hands close to his neck, feeling the stiffness there course through her fingers. After twenty minutes, she gave her hands a shake and walked to the end of the table to spend the last bit of time on his feet.

"All done," she announced. "I would recommend sitting up slowly."

He did as instructed, opening his eyes and taking a deep breath.

"Good. Just sit for a few minutes. How does it feel?"

"I can't feel anything. I don't know what you did but the pain's gone from my back."

"Excellent. I'm not pushing you into this. However, I think you would benefit from another session. Your neck and shoulders could do with more work."

He stepped off the table and sat in the chair to put his shoes back on. When he stood again, he just grinned, like a six-year-old who'd been given an ice cream. "Well, I have to say, I didn't really believe in this an hour ago. But, yes. I'll book in again. Is next Thursday okay?"

"We usually recommend a week between treatments."

"Unfortunately I'm flying to New York on Friday."

"Okay. Thursday's good, then."

As she walked him out to reception, he asked, "What do I owe you?"

"Nothing. The almost-family discount for you, Mr Bowen."

"Brad, please." He shook her hand. "See you next week. And thank you."

Jay returned to her office to make notes on the session. At least she'd made one member of the Bowen family happy. She checked the time. Friday afternoons were generally appointment-free so she could make an early getaway for the drive to Norfolk. Today she was meeting Josh at the tailor's to pick up the suits. He'd been crestfallen when she told him the wedding was off, but she didn't see any reason he couldn't still have the suit. There would be other occasions for him to wear it.

†

Deuce

Amanda found she was enjoying the trip more than she could have expected. Unknown to her, Lynne had booked them a junior suite on the ferry that sailed between Barcelona and Rome. The twenty-one hour journey was a treat in itself. Lynne explained that the train would have taken a few hours longer and not been as comfortable.

She lay on the bed in their hotel room, images swirling through her mind from their tour of the city earlier in the day…the Colosseum, the Forum, Trevi Fountain…finally collapsing onto the Spanish Steps to revel in the warm weather and watch other tourists passing by. For several hours, Amanda had managed to forget that this was supposed to be her wedding day.

Lynne emerged from the bathroom, rubbing her hair dry. The hotel bathrobe gaped open, revealing her rounded breasts and a triangle of pubic hair, neatly trimmed. Amanda felt a tug of desire and immediately tamped it down. No, she shouldn't even think about it. Had it really only been all about sex with Jay? She could talk to Lynne about anything. But when had she shared any meaningful conversation with Jay?

†

Jay towelled off after her shower. The run through the Holland Park trails left her feeling refreshed. Not as good as a run along the beach at the cottage, though. She thought Ritchie agreed. He'd been restless the evening before, no doubt wondering why they weren't going to Norfolk on a Friday evening.

She would have liked to be there too on this, her non-wedding day. But she'd agreed to meet Dougie and Josh for lunch. It would be a while before they saw Dougie again. He was flying out to Alaska on Monday and would be there for months.

Josh had been semi-relieved when she told him the wedding was cancelled. He had been looking forward to wearing the suit for the ceremony, being in charge of the rings. But he confessed to having trouble writing a best-man's speech and had worried about making an idiot of himself at the reception when called on to say something. Jay told him she was sure Dougie would have stepped in to make some highly inappropriate comments about her past.

He was also stunned when Jay told him the mews house was now in his name.

"But why?" He had clutched her arm. "You're not going anywhere, are you?"

"No, not at all. I've been thinking about doing this for some time."

"But that was probably because you were going to move in with Amanda after you got married. This is too much, Mum. The house is worth millions."

Jay placed her hand on top of his. "Your happiness is worth that and more to me. When you find someone to share your life with, I'll move out. Maybe sell the cottage and buy a place nearer to London."

That had caused another shocked look to cross his face. "You wouldn't sell the cottage, surely."

"I don't know. Another feeling that's been growing for a while. Time to let go of Charley, perhaps."

Now as she walked down the street towards the restaurant, she wondered if she really could ever truly let go.

†

Deuce

Tess checked her watch under the table. No messages from either Donna or Alice. Her instructions were to keep Cheryl out of the way until everyone was in place. Alice had promised to be there, having taken her party clothes to work. Her shift had ended half an hour ago, so Tess thought she would be in time to take her place with the rest of the crowd waiting at the golf club.

"Bored with my company already, darling?" Cheryl finished her drink.

"No. I just thought Alice would be joining us."

"Is she still enjoying the job?"

"Mostly. But she has been talking about applying to the real police force. Now she's got a taste for it."

"How do you feel about that?"

"Worried. She says she'll feel safer. Wearing the proper gear and having backup. I can't help thinking about the increase of shootings and stabbings everywhere."

"Well, I guess you know you won't be able to stop her if she has her heart set on it."

"Yeah, I just wish she'd settled on a less dangerous career."

"Nothing's safe these days. I'm glad I finished teaching when I did."

"Do you want another?" Tess waved her glass.

"No. I think I better pace myself." Cheryl grinned. "How long before you take me to wherever this surprise party is?"

Tess rocked back in her seat. "How did you know?"

"After forty years, I know when my wife is keeping something from me. She's been acting weird for weeks now."

Tess laughed. "Fine. Donna's going to text me to let me know when everyone's there. Can you at least manage to act surprised?"

"No problem. Teaching is a lot like acting."

Cheryl played her part to perfection, the look of shock giving way to delight, as she entered the room full of people shouting, "Surprise" and "Happy Birthday." Watching her dancing with Donna afterwards, Tess felt a sudden rush of affection for the two women who had never wavered in their love for her. Even at her most difficult. She was embarrassed now when she looked back at her teenage self.

Running away at fourteen had been a particular low point. Tess wasn't proud of the pain she'd caused them in the ten hours she was missing before the traffic cops picked her up at the side of the road where she'd been trying to hitchhike. The police officer's bollocking had been harsher than anything her parents said to her. Their drawn tear-stained faces were the only reproach as they met her at the door and embraced her in a three-way hug.

Tess didn't want to see that look again. But she knew she was pushing it with her obsession of finding out what she could about Charlotte Summersbridge. Perhaps there was nothing more to discover. Time to let it go and give all her attention to the real live women in her life.

"Are you going to dance with me, or do I have to wait until I'm sixty-five?" Alice stood in front of her, holding out her hand expectantly.

"Yes...and no." Tess grasped it and let her girlfriend lead her to the dance floor.

CHAPTER TEN

Jay finished writing up the file on her last client of the day. It was only one o'clock, but she'd kept the afternoon clear to meet Josh at the tattoo parlour for the final inking. The weekend in London had left her feeling restless and out of sorts. She checked her appointments, wondering if she could manage to take off on Thursday afternoon.

The intercom buzzed just as she was putting her jacket on. One arm in a sleeve, she stabbed the button.

"Sorry, Jay. There's two people here to see you. From the Danish embassy."

"Okay. I'll meet them in here."

She had treated embassy staff before. The clinic's proximity to the cluster of embassies in Kensington and Knightsbridge made it the first choice for anyone not wanting to travel far. Jay only hoped they weren't going to upset her afternoon plans by asking her to fit someone important in for an appointment, like their ambassador or a visiting dignitary.

A man and a woman appeared in the hallway, casually dressed. She knew from previous dealings with Danes that this didn't necessarily mean they weren't on official business. They both produced ID badges on which the Danish flag was recognisable along with their photos and names...Hilde Pedersen and Olaf Jensen.

"You are Julie Ann Reid?" the woman asked.

"Yes. But please call me Jay." She ushered them into the room. "Would you like something to drink? Tea or coffee?"

"No thank you." Again, it was the woman who spoke.

They sat side by side on the couch, and Jay took the chair next to it. This was where she seated clients on their first consultation. Less formal than sitting behind a desk.

The woman took the lead once more, her English only slightly accented. "Please accept our apologies for not making an appointment. We require some information which is urgent."

"Okay. Glad to help, if I can." She couldn't think what assistance she could give them that required urgent attention. If it were simply another embassy official needing treatment they would just have phoned ahead rather than turning up in person.

"We were directed here by one of our colleagues at the embassy. You see, we are trying to trace anyone who is related to Charlotte Summersbridge."

A lump arose in Jay's throat. She managed to croak out, "You've found her?"

The man spoke up for the first time. "The wreck of the research ship has been found. We are anxious to confirm the identities of the remains of the people who were onboard."

Deuce

"Remains?"

"I'm sorry. There are only bones left." He looked to his partner for help.

"Skeletons," she added, for unnecessary clarification.

Jay struggled to find her voice. "Where was the ship found?"

"Just off the Faroe Islands."

"But...they weren't going that far north, I'm sure. Charley told me they were covering the North Sea, well, near Denmark actually. Are you sure it's the same ship?"

The two officials looked at each other, clearly uncomfortable. The woman spoke again. "They must have experienced bad weather to be blown off course. The photographs provided by the dive team show that the vessel was severely damaged. Not just wear and tear from having lain at the bottom of the sea for so long. And yes, the name on the hull is *RV Caspian*, registered in Bermuda."

The man continued, "Our colleagues thought you must have some connection with Charlotte, as the clinic here is named after her. We haven't been able to trace any relatives in order to match DNA with the bones that have been retrieved."

"She didn't know her parents. They abandoned her. But she does have a child."

"Yes, she told us she gave birth to two children."

In that split second, Jay had decided to give them Tess. She didn't know if the hormones Josh took had skewed his DNA.

"You could try Tess Bailey-Roberts. Charley gave her up for adoption. She's about thirty years old."

"Do you have an address for her?"

"No. I do have her phone number, though." Jay opened the Contacts list on her phone and read Tess's number to them.

The man tapped it into his phone. "Does she live in London?"

"I'm not sure where, but she works in the city. So possibly not too far away."

They stood up together, and Jay walked them to the door. "Will you let me know if there's a match?" She couldn't help the tears that threatened. "It's been hard not knowing...."

The woman patted her arm. "Yes, of course. And thank you."

Jay collapsed into the chair once the door closed and gave in to the tears now streaming down her face. Her mobile's ringtone brought her back to the present. Josh's image lit up the screen.

"Are you still coming?"

"Yes. Sorry, just a last-minute thing. I'm leaving now."

†

After the visit from the Danes, Tess couldn't concentrate on the article she was writing. The DNA swab had only taken a minute and they hadn't given her much information during that time. Nothing new came up on a Google search of either Charlotte or the ship's name. They'd been remarkably successful in keeping the discovery quiet. She tried Jay's phone, but she wasn't answering. When she called the clinic, the receptionist said Jay was gone for the day.

She googled the names of the two embassy officials, but both names were so common, there were thousands of hits for Olaf Jensen and Hilde Pedersen. Should she have checked their credentials more closely? Maybe it was some kind of cruel scam.

Tess shut down her computer, grabbed her coat, and left the office. No one stopped her. They would assume she had a lead for a story. She walked aimlessly for a while. Alice was working and wouldn't be home until late that evening. Cheryl and Donna were away on a two-day golf break at a hotel somewhere in Derbyshire…a continuation of Cheryl's birthday celebrations. But she needed to talk to someone. That someone had to be Jay. With a more purposeful stride, she changed direction and merged with the crowd of commuters and tourists heading for the Oxford Circus tube station. She could cope with the nose-to-armpit journey for the four stops before Notting Hill Gate. It was only a short walk to Jay's house from there.

At the last moment, unable to bear the heat and the odours in the crowded carriage, Tess shoved her way out onto the platform at Queensway. She craved fresh air, as the lift to the street level was as crowded as the train, and walked across the road to Kensington Gardens.

†

Jay laid her head on the back of the sofa and closed her eyes. She felt Ritchie's wet nose nudging her hand. He always knew when she was in need of comfort. Opening her eyes, she smiled down at him and stroked his upturned belly.

Josh placed a glass of red wine on the table in front of her and sat opposite holding a bottle of Peroni. "So are you going to tell me what's up? You've been very quiet all afternoon."

"I'm always quiet, aren't I?"

"This is a different kind of quiet."

"Okay, Sherlock." Jay sat up and took a sip of wine. She put the glass carefully back on the table. Ritchie rolled over and made himself comfortable next to her as if he, too, were waiting for her confession. "Just before I left the clinic today, I was visited by two Danish embassy officials." She recounted the reason for their visit, trying to keep her voice from shaking.

"Wow! That's amazing. How did they find the ship after all this time?"

"I don't know. They didn't say. In fact, they were a bit cagey about the whole thing."

"Maybe it was treasure hunters. Just happened to spot the wreck and thought there would be valuable stuff down there."

The doorbell rang.

Josh put his beer down and stood. "Are you expecting anyone?"

"No."

"Okay. I'll see who it is."

Ritchie jumped off the sofa and scampered after him down the stairs. A few minutes later, Jay heard two sets of feet plus Ritchie's paws coming back up. When she saw the person who followed Josh into the room, somehow she wasn't surprised.

"Tess. Would you like a glass of wine?" The girl looked weary.

"I'm on it." Josh was already heading for the kitchen.

"I'm sorry I didn't have a chance to warn you. I gather they were on the phone to you before they left the clinic."

Josh returned with the drink for Tess. She'd seated herself in the other armchair.

"Thanks." She took a large gulp. "I couldn't settle to anything after they left. I've been walking around all afternoon and ended up sitting for a while in the Princess Diana Memorial Garden. I hope you don't mind, but when I realised how close I was to here...."

"Not a problem." Jay smiled at her. "I've only just filled Josh in about it."

"They didn't tell me much. Just took the swab and left."

"I didn't get much from them either."

"There's nothing on the Internet about finding the ship."

"Well they did say they were keeping a lid on it until all the relatives had been contacted and they were able to establish the identities from the bones recovered." Jay took a sip from her glass. "Hence the need for a DNA sample."

"Finding the wreck after all this time. It's unbelievable."

Tess voiced the thought that had been in her mind for the last few hours. Jay closed her eyes again and tried to block out the images that had been haunting her since the visit from the Danes. Could Charley still be alive? She gave herself a mental shake. That just wasn't possible. She would drive herself crazy if she started to believe that.

†

Amanda tried to relax as Lynne drove the hire car around another bend of the coast road. She closed her eyes to shut out the proximity of the cliff edge and the surging sea below.

Corsica was beautiful, and she was sure she would enjoy it once they reached their destination. She looked forward to sitting by the hotel pool with a cocktail in her hand. Perhaps then she could forget Jay should have been here.

It wasn't fair to Lynne, who had been the perfect companion for the past week. How much longer would she put up with Amanda's bouts of self-pity? She was going to try, really try, to enjoy this week. A whole six days of freedom before returning to the wreckage of her life in London.

"You can open your eyes now."

The car came to a stop and Amanda stared out at a gorgeous vista, the sun throwing early evening rays across a calm expanse of water. "Lovely," she murmured, releasing her seat belt.

"Let's get checked in. I know I could do with a drink."

As they walked up the marble steps to the hotel entrance, Amanda tapped Lynne's arm. "Thank you for being here."

Lynne stopped to take in the view again. "The pleasure is all mine. This is an amazing place."

Amanda stopped herself in time from saying, *Jay chose it*. Jay was history. She wasn't going to spoil this week either for herself or Lynne by mentioning her name again.

PART THREE

CHAPTER ELEVEN

I am Charlotte Summersbridge. This is my mantra now. I repeat the name over and over when I wake each morning as the memories surge forward with the force of an oncoming tide, wave after wave. I would like to be able to hold back the tide as in the story of King Canute, although he was in truth trying to demonstrate the opposite.

So much has changed, so much remains the same. Newspapers regurgitating the usual conflicts…with EU bureaucracy, another war zone in the Middle East, Russian spies killed on the streets. The main difference I see now is that everyone has a voice. These Internet sites…Facebook, Twitter, personal blogs, YouTube…some of it good, some bad.

I read every newspaper delivered to the embassy as I wait. Waiting for my life to resume. My Danish hosts are very gracious. Even though I feel I'm a great nuisance to them, they treat me well. Unlike that man hiding in the Ecuadorean embassy a few streets away, I can go out without fear of arrest. Although my hosts insist I have someone with me at all times. I am a stateless person until my "death" can be reversed.

How does it feel to come back from the dead? Hilde asks me this as we walk through Hyde Park. She is my minder most days. Walking along the once-familiar paths, I ponder this question. Each day I recover more memories from the past, recalling a Charlotte Summersbridge I once knew. As each one comes into focus, I'm overwhelmed with a tidal wave of emotions. Particularly when I remember Jay.

I want to see Jay. But I'm afraid. After twenty-three years, she will have moved on with her life. And Julie, our baby. She's never known me and will now be a young woman. My other daughter, Tess, may have vague memories of me from her early childhood. But I have no right to intrude on her life. I left her in good hands with my former biology teacher and her partner.

But I want answers too. How did Jay cope with looking after a baby? She probably gave her up for adoption. Then she could have carried on with her tennis career. I know she said she would cut back on touring to be with the child and me, but I always felt I was holding her back from what she loved to do. I'm afraid to ask. I've deliberately not searched for Jay on the Internet even though I gather you can find out anything about anyone by just typing in a name. As long as they have a digital footprint. Another new expression I've learned.

I could ask Hilde about Jay. But I don't. In answer to her question, I just say I'm still processing it. We reach

Speaker's Corner and turn around. One day soon, I may be able to face walking down Oxford Street. But right now I can't handle being in a crowd. The legacy, I suppose, of living in a small fishing village all this time. My pseudo-life as Katrin Nielsen. Fished from the sea.

At my low points, I wish I had perished with the others. How did I survive? Their faces come to me in the night.

Before returning to the embassy, we stop at a coffee shop. It's not very busy, and Hilde guides me to a corner table, knowing my need to feel secure, my back to the wall.

I look at my hands while Hilde fetches the coffee. No longer the hands of an academic. Weathered by more than age, years of gutting fish, harvesting vegetables. It was only in the last two years I had relief from these tasks with taking on the work of setting up the small library in the village.

I feel sick now when I think of all the whale meat I have eaten. Charlotte Summersbridge would never have consumed anything from a sea mammal.

"I do not wish to press you," Hilde says after taking a tentative sip of her drink. A latte, she tells me. So many names for coffee are listed on the board behind the counter. I had asked for a black coffee. I heard her say americano, no milk, when she ordered. Her drink looks like it contains more milk than coffee.

Her opening question isn't unexpected. I feel she has been waiting for me to speak of it first.

"Do you think you are ready to meet Jay Reid, or one of your daughters?"

I look down at the murky depths of the coffee; my hands grip the mug tightly. She waits patiently for an answer, as always.

"Jay. I know I need to see Jay."

†

Jay stood to greet the Danish official who entered her office. Hilde Pedersen, she recalled the name now.
"Thank you for seeing me."
"I thought there were two of you."
"Ah, yes. I just need a moment to advise you of some developments."
Jay came out from behind her desk and waved her to the seating area, but Hilde didn't move. "You have the DNA results."
"Yes. We have matched the DNA of all the ship's crew with living relatives." Hilde raised her hand to stop Jay from speaking. "We now know more about what happened. There is a survivor who has been living on one of the Faroe Islands. Loss of memory prevented them from coming forward before now."
"This person is here with you?"
"Yes. I will give you some time together." She left the room.
When the door opened again, Jay felt her legs turn to liquid. "Charley?" she managed to croak out before collapsing onto the sofa.
"I'm sorry. I thought Hilde told you." The Charley-like apparition seated herself in the chair opposite Jay.
"Just that someone survived. How…?" Jay couldn't find the words. The woman in front of her was Charley, but not Charley. Her hair was a darker red and shorter, her face and hands coarsened—by living on a wind-battered island, perhaps. Jay thought the Faroe Islands to be like Orkney or Shetland, but wilder. Only the eyes held the intensity she remembered.

"I don't know how I escaped the same fate as my shipmates. I'm experiencing flashbacks of the storm that drove us off course. The storm that destroyed our communication and navigation equipment. But beyond that, nothing. I realise I must have been thrown clear as the boat started to sink. I must have swum to the shore where I was found. That memory hasn't returned."

Jay listened closely as Charley recounted the day her memory of a previous life came back and her struggle to come to terms with the amount of time that had passed.

"I thought, at first, that I should let it stay in the past. I had lived as Katrin Nielsen for all those years. I have a son, Konrad. But then as more memories surfaced, I thought of those who would think I was dead. You, my two daughters. Maybe Tess has forgotten me. I left her in good hands. And our baby, Julie, wouldn't know me. But I knew I wanted to know how things turned out with you and the girls. Did you keep the baby? Or did you give her up for adoption?"

The smile that creased her face then sent a searing pain through Jay. It was Charley's smile.

"I can't see the Jay I knew looking after a baby."

"I did look after our baby. Having that responsibility when you disappeared was what kept me going. And I've seen Tess a few times recently. She was curious about her birth mother."

"She is well?"

"Yes. She's a journalist."

"And Julie?" Charley leant forward in her seat.

"Before starting kindergarten, Julie wanted to be called Jules." Jay hesitated. She didn't know how she was going to tell Charley about Julie's transition to Josh. "Academically bright, like her mother, and working as an architect now."

Jay stood and retrieved the photo frame she kept on her desk. She handed it to Charley. "The two most important people in my life."

Charley studied the photos briefly. "I recognise myself as I looked years ago. But who's the boy?"

"That's Julie. Now Josh. He always knew from a young age that he was born in the wrong body."

"You let my baby have a sex change?"

"I didn't let him. It's what he wanted. It's called transitioning nowadays."

Charley looked at the photo again. Jay thought it was a good one of Josh, taken only a few years ago, smiling into the camera, happy and relaxed.

"Oh God, I can't believe this. I should never have come back. I would have trusted you with my life. My baby's life. And you've done this. Created an abomination!" She dumped the frame on the table and stormed out of the room.

Jay followed, in time to hear Charley tell a startled Hilde that she would wait for her outside.

"What is the problem?" Hilde asked Jay.

"It's complicated." Jay took one of her business cards out of her pocket and wrote the address for the mews house, and her personal mobile number on the back. "When she calms down, maybe she would like to visit me at home."

Hilde took the card. "What happened?"

"Perhaps you can explain to her that gender reassignment is more commonly accepted now. She's upset to find out that her baby daughter has transitioned. Josh has been living as a male since before puberty."

"Ah. I see. That could be difficult for her to accept."

"We've both had a shock today. But one thing hasn't changed."

"What is that?"

"Her quick temper. We always argued, a lot."

Jay returned to her office and shut the door. She sank back down on the sofa. What did she expect after twenty-three years? The woman she knew as Charley had lived a different life for all that time. She picked the photo up off the table, where it had landed face down. The glass had cracked, a jagged line now separating Charley and Josh. A sign from the cosmos. After seeing her lover return from the dead, maybe it was time to start believing in the supernatural. The glass in the frame could be easily replaced, but it was going to take longer to repair their lost relationship. After Charley's reaction just now, Jay wasn't sure that was possible.

Setting the frame gently back on the table, she rested her head on the back of the sofa and let the tears flow.

†

I wait for Hilde on the steps outside the clinic. As soon as she comes out, I start walking and she hurries to catch up.

"Katrin, slow down."

She hasn't got used to calling me Charlotte. I'm hardly used to thinking of myself as Charlotte. I slow my pace and we walk in silence. It's a longer walk than perhaps Hilde would like, but she stays with me. Sometimes I wonder how she feels about being my minder. Does she mind? I haven't even met a Faroese representative yet. There is someone based here in London, but they must be on holiday. I should be their problem, not Denmark's.

We go back through Hyde Park, retracing our steps from earlier. As we near the embassy, I ask if we can stop in the gardens at Hans Place.

Deuce

We sit side by side on a bench, and I find my voice. "Julie was a beautiful baby. I remember holding her in my arms for the first time. Jay was there too. I was so happy. This would be the start of our family."

Hilde doesn't say anything.

"How could she let this happen? Is it even legal?"

She doesn't ask what I'm talking about. Jay must have told her why I ran out. Finally she says, "Yes, it's perfectly legal." Hilde puts a hand on my arm and turns her head to face me. "I think this has all been too much for you today." She stands and I follow her obediently.

Later, sitting on the bed in the room allocated to me, I think about Jay. I would have recognised her immediately. She has aged well. A few more lines around the eyes and mouth, but the same body shape, lean and sinewy. I wonder if she still plays tennis. She was so good on the court. I can see her in my mind's eye, stretching to hit a ball, grace and beauty combined.

What did she think of me? I look nothing like that photo she keeps on her desk. My hair colour has faded from the bright red of my youth to a duller hue with flecks of grey. Redheads aren't supposed to go grey.

†

Josh threw his arms around her and held on tight. Something he hadn't done in years. After a few moments of fierce hugging, he let go and collapsed onto the sofa.

"Is it really Charley? I can't believe it."

"It is definitely her."

"You don't seem too happy about it." He studied her face closely as she sat opposite.

"She's different."

"Well, I guess she would be." Josh pulled out his phone. "Where exactly are the Faroe Islands?"

"A long way from where their boat should have been." Jay ran her fingers through her hair. "I need to talk to Mo, sort out the finances."

"Is the cottage hers?"

"It was originally. But we put it in both our names before you were born. And I was able to pay off the mortgage with some of my tennis winnings."

"When can I meet her? Does Tess know?"

"I don't know the answer to either of those questions. Charley's still adjusting to the way things have changed while she's been away. Her memories of how things were will likely conflict with how they are now." Jay thought this described her own state of mind.

"How did she look?"

"Older."

"Obviously. Can you be more specific?"

"Just older. Her hair colour isn't so bright, more lines on her face, but the same smile. She has another child, a son. I don't know how that happened. I guess there was a man involved, but we didn't get a chance to talk much."

"So she might not remember she was a lesbian?"

Before Jay could respond, her phone rang. She picked it up. No caller ID but it was a London number. When she answered, she recognised the voice right away.

"Yes, of course. She'll need to speak to my business manager, Mo Farrell." Jay rattled off the number and then repeated it for Hilde. The next question wasn't really a surprise, either. "I'm sure that can be arranged. Mo has a key."

Josh looked at her, eyebrows raised as she ended the call.

"That was Hilde Pedersen from the embassy. Charley's asking about money and she also wants to go to the cottage."

"Hey, that's great. We should call Tess and we can have a family reunion there."

Jay didn't want to burst his excited bubble just yet, but he would have to know eventually. "I don't think that's a good idea. From what I saw of her today, she's still a bit fragile. Coming to terms with all the memories that are surfacing."

"But we can tell Tess, can't we?"

"I'm not sure she's that keen to meet her yet. Charley only asked if she was well and didn't seem that interested in the answer."

"Well if you don't call her, I will."

"Okay, okay. I agree she needs to know. I just don't want her to rush into journo mode, wanting to spread the story immediately."

"I'm sure she wouldn't do that."

Jay wasn't so sure, but she picked up her phone and took it into the kitchen to make the call.

†

"You'll wear the carpet out, Tess. There's no point worrying. She'll see you when she wants to see you."

Alice's tone was calm, but that only wound Tess up tighter.

"Why doesn't she want to see me now?"

"If she's just remembering who she is after twenty-three years, I should think it's a lot to take in."

"But I'm her daughter." Tess sank down on the sofa and let Alice draw her into an embrace.

"Well, from what you've told me, it sounds like she's not keen on seeing Jay or Josh either."

"But I need to see her." Tess pushed her away and sat up. "The story will break and I should be the one who gets in first. This will be big."

"So you want to use your connection to expose her to the world." Alice's eyes bored into her. "I don't think you're seeing this too clearly. You're part of the story. Journos will be knocking on your door wanting the inside goss. And don't forget, you'll be selling out Donna and Cheryl too."

"I'm not going to be 'selling out' anyone. This is a family story. My family."

Alice got up and started pacing, covering the same length of carpet Tess had been treading. "What about those other families? The relatives of the ones who didn't survive. I don't think the social-media trolls are going to treat Charlotte Summersbridge too kindly. How was it that she was able to swim ashore? Isn't this memory loss a bit convenient? What's she been doing for twenty-three years? Was it guilt that made her stay away so long?"

"Guilt about what?"

"Well, that's what we don't know. But these questions will be asked."

"You make it sound like she'll be on trial."

"Oh, it will be a trial, believe me. Trial by media." Alice knelt in front of Tess and took her hands. Tears were trickling out of her eyes. "And I don't want to see you get hurt. Yes, this woman's your birth mother. But she doesn't know you, any more than you know her. You have a real family, the parents who have loved you for thirty years. Can't you see how devastating this will be for them when you announce to the world that you're Charlotte's daughter?"

The force of Alice's words took Tess aback. Her own tears started. "But she did know me. She used to visit."

"Yes, but you were very young when she disappeared. She didn't see you growing up. She doesn't know the person you are now. She doesn't know anything about you."

"I still want to see her."

"It will be like meeting a stranger. Jay was her lover and it doesn't sound like she's been able to connect with her, so why would you be any different?"

Alice stood and pulled Tess to her feet. She held her close, waiting patiently for Tess's breathing to calm. It was something she was good at, often pulling Tess back from the brink of making rash decisions. Tess sometimes wondered how Alice put up with her; they were complete opposites in many ways.

Chapter Twelve

The view from the cottage is the same. I stand looking out to the wide horizon. Not unlike the vista I had all those years on Suðuroy. Just flatter, tamer somehow. Taking a deep breath of the sea air, I turn to look at the building that was once my home, my refuge. The addition of a conservatory is tastefully done, and I walk inside.

I hear the sounds from the kitchen. Mo left me staring at the sea and came in to put the coffee on. I walk through to this room I spent a lot of time in. As with everything since I came back, it's not quite how I remember it.

Mo turns away from the counter. "The coffee will be ready in a few minutes. I've put the groceries away."

"Thank you."

"Do you want to be on your own now?"

We discussed this on the way here. Mo offered to stay nearby at the pub. It sounds so Greta Garbo, telling her I want to be alone. But I need to try to reconnect with the memories stored here. Although I try pushing it away, the desire to find my way back to Jay keeps surfacing.

"Not yet. Please stay for coffee, at least."

I see that Mo has brought my backpack in as well. It contains my meagre possessions, a few clothes and books. My new phone.

Mo pours the coffee, places a mug in front of me, and sits when she's added milk and sugar to her own.

"Jay said she changed the sheets before she left last time."

"Does she come here often?"

"Yes. Every weekend."

"Oh." I feel a tug of guilt. My presence is keeping her from enjoying her weekend retreat. "It's a long way from the city."

"That seems to be what she likes about it. They held a vigil for you every year on the beach."

"They?"

"Jay and Josh. Dougie whenever he was in the country."

Dougie. Another name from the past. "Where is he now?"

"In Alaska, last I heard."

"Does he know…about my…return?"

"Jay contacted him. But he won't be able to leave for another six weeks."

"Did he…?" I'm not sure how to word this. "Was he around much while Julie was growing up?"

"On and off."

"Wasn't he able to stop Julie from making this change?"

"Look, Charlotte, you really need to take this up with Josh. He's an adult, and although it's been a shock for you,

you're going to need to accept him now as your son, if you want to have any relationship with him."

Tears spring to my eyes. "I have a son. I thought I had two daughters."

Mo seems uncomfortable. I try to control my emotions and wipe away the tears. She changes the subject, talking about the weather and the lack of visitors at this time of year. The beach, she tells me, will be empty. Just how I like it. She leaves after finishing her coffee. I hear the car drive away. A hire car. Mo didn't think I'd appreciate the long journey on the back of her motorbike. Maybe I would have liked that if it hadn't been raining.

Wandering into the living room, I light the fire that's been pre-laid. By Jay, I guess. It was her habit to always leave the fireplace ready, primed for the next visit. While the logs catch fire, I stand in front of the mantelpiece and examine the photographs. Me, the same one Jay has on her desk. A more recent photo of her with the man I know as Dougie—Julie's sperm donor—and the young person who is, or was, my baby daughter. They look happy.

I go into the bedroom and place my bag on the bed. This room is mainly unchanged. I loved waking here. With or without Jay beside me. The mornings with Jay didn't allow for quiet contemplation. Months spent apart meant most of our time together was taken exploring each other's bodies. Did she still want to explore mine? Or has that ship sailed, and sunk?

My body, dragged from the depths. That night of terror haunts my sleep now. Increasingly clear…the howling wind, the waves crashing over the bows. Then nothing but the pounding in my head, my limbs like lead, but somehow I keep moving until I arrive, battered and beached on a sandy shore, like a seal.

Struggling, as I did then to clamber onto a rock out of the reach of the oncoming waves, I make myself open a closet door.

†

Jay waved her hand to indicate Ross should sit on the sofa. When Sandra, the clinic's receptionist, came in, she sat next to him. They eyed her nervously as she seated herself in the chair opposite.

"I'm taking some time off. A week, maybe two."

"Are you okay?" Sandra asked.

Ross had already enquired after her health, although in a less subtle way, telling her she looked like shit.

"I'm not ill. I just need to sort out a few personal things." *Like a dead lover coming back to life.* "I hope it won't come to this, but it may be necessary to close the clinic for a while."

"Why?" Ross obviously hadn't been expecting her to say this.

"Charlotte Summersbridge isn't dead."

Sandra made the connection first. "Those Danish people who came here the second time. Was that her? The one who rushed out looking angry."

Jay nodded and launched into the story of where Charley had been and her recently recovered memory.

"I don't understand." Ross shifted in his seat. "Why would we have to close? Doesn't she want her name associated with the clinic?"

"Most of our clients don't know what the initials stand for. We're just CSC to them. No, it's the press interest this story may generate that worries me. You'll be in the front line, Sandra, and if they can't get any answers by calling, they may use the tactic of booking appointments to talk to staff."

"What should I say when anyone asks?"

"Refer them to the Danish embassy."

"I thought the Faroes were independent of Denmark."

"They are. But the premises in London also house the Iceland embassy and representatives for the Faroe Islands." Jay gave Ross a wry smile. "I looked it up."

The phone on her desk rang. Sandra moved to get up, but Jay said, "I'll get it."

"Sorry, I routed the calls through as I didn't know how long we'd be."

"That's okay." Jay picked up the receiver. "CSC. Jay Reid here. How can I help you?"

The voice on the other end was young and sounded uncertain. "Hello. I am looking for my mother. Is she here?"

"I'm sorry, you must have the wrong number."

"My name is Konrad."

"Oh." The name and the carefully spoken words jolted Jay's memory. "Where are you?"

"I am here, outside. May I come in?"

"Yes. I'll be right there."

Jay put the phone down. "Bloody hell. Charley's son has turned up. I'll go and let him in. It's opening time anyway."

Sandra and Ross followed her out.

The boy standing on the steps didn't look very old, maybe thirteen or fourteen, but Jay would have known he was Charley's offspring right away. He and Josh could have been twins. Except that Konrad looked cold and famished, and had probably slept in the same clothes for several nights.

She ushered him into her office, and without being asked, Sandra appeared with coffee for both of them and a plate of chocolate digestives. Jay waited for Konrad to settle. He ate two biscuits in quick succession and gulped down some coffee.

"Thank you."

"You're welcome. You know that your mother is most likely to be at the Danish embassy."

"Yes. But I cannot go there."

After a few false starts, Jay got the story out of him. He had been left in the care of a family in Copenhagen. Once his mother had sorted out her identity, then he would be able to join her. But he had no passport.

"How did you get here?"

"On a boat."

"Won't this family have reported you missing?"

"They think I visit with a school friend."

Jay watched him eat another biscuit. Should she phone Hilde? That would be the sensible thing to do. He looked so vulnerable, though. So like Josh at that age, wavering between a boy and a man. The boy was dominant now, and Konrad looked like he was most in need of a good meal, rather than a grilling from Danish officials.

She swept her eyes around the room. Her desk was clear, everything tidied away in preparation for her leave of absence, however long that may be. She'd even tucked the photos of Charley and Josh in a locked drawer. To protect them or herself, she wasn't sure which. And now, Konrad. The unspoken plea was there in his eyes.

Standing, she picked up her jacket and phone. "Come on. I think you could do with a good meal."

He followed her out, and Jay stopped at the reception desk. "If anyone asks, he hasn't been here."

Sandra nodded. "Have a good break."

"Thanks. But do call if there's anything you need help with." Jay didn't need to spell it out. Sandra knew what she meant.

"Go on. Relax. We'll be fine here."

Jay walked out of the clinic with Konrad, wondering when she would start feeling fine again.

†

Mo deposited her overnight bag on the bed. The Sextant's bedrooms were undergoing a winter refurbishment, so the landlord had booked her in at the B & B across the road. In a way she was pleased. The bedroom was cleaner and brighter than any she had stayed in before at the pub. Their rooms were in dire need of updating.

She wondered how Charlotte was settling in at the cottage. Although she'd been managing Jay's business affairs since her first year on the tennis circuit, Mo had never met the love of Jay's life before. She didn't recognise this version of Charley from Jay's descriptions.

Jay was also clearly having a problem matching her memories of the woman she'd loved with the real-life one now. Mo thought back to their uncomfortable meeting earlier that day.

"I'm sorry, Jay." Mo watched Jay pacing back and forth in her office. "She asked me to take her there."

"Great. She must want your company more than mine."

"She's still adjusting."

"And how long is that going to take? Another twenty-three years?"

"It can't be easy coming back from the dead."
"Maybe she should have stayed dead."
"You don't mean that."

Jay's shoulders had slumped, her whole bearing taking on the one Mo recognised from when she was defeated on a tennis court. She had always bounced back with renewed determination from those bouts, though. Mo wasn't so sure she would recover from this one so easily.

Her phone rang just as she was about to step in the bath. Mo thought of ignoring the insistent ringing but then realised it could be Charlotte, unable to find something at the cottage. Wrapping the bath towel around her shivering body, she returned to the bedroom and answered the call, surprised to see it was Jay.

"We have a problem."

Mo sat on the bed and gripped the phone tightly. She hoped it wasn't a financial issue, as she couldn't do much about it away from her office.

"What's up?"
"Konrad."
"Who?"
"Charley's son. He was supposed to stay in Copenhagen while she sorted out things here. But he hitched a ride on a fishing trawler. And somehow was able to find the clinic. His English isn't very good, but he's managed pretty well so far."

"Oh. Um, why didn't he go to the embassy?"
"He doesn't have a passport and didn't want to get sent back."
"Where is he now?"
"Here. At home."
"So, you're harbouring an illegal immigrant."

"Come on, Mo. I can't report him. He just wants to see his mum."

Mo walked back into the bathroom. It was warmer in there but she suspected her bath water was cooling rapidly.

"It's too late to do anything this evening. Charlotte made it clear she wants some time alone in the cottage. And knowing he's here will worry her. Why not keep him there for a few days, show him the sights?"

"Fine. He and Josh seem to be getting on. Tess has been agitating as well, though, wanting to know why Charley doesn't want to see her."

"I know it's hard, but everyone needs to stay calm. I'll talk to Charlotte tomorrow before setting off. And we'll discuss things when I get back."

"I hope you've told her to keep a low profile. I'm sure the story's about to break. Tess hinted at it."

Mo poked the water with her toe. Still warm enough. "I don't think she's planning on going anywhere other than a walk along the beach. Not likely to meet any visitors at this time of year."

After ending the call, Mo added some more hot water to the tub, then sank gratefully into the warmth with the bubbles reaching her chin. No point worrying about things that hadn't happened yet. Jay was right to be concerned about the impending news coverage, though. Mo was struck by the thought that even with Charlotte's coldness towards her, Jay's overriding instinct was to protect her from harm.

†

Lynne let the cats out of their respective carriers. Babs had complained loudly all the way back from the cattery.

Slinky satisfied himself with giving her the evil eye whenever she looked at him.

Leaving them in the kitchen with bowls of food and water, she peeked into the bedroom. Amanda was still asleep, light snuffles coming from under the duvet. She shut the door again and went into the living room. After rebooting the Wi-Fi and fetching herself a glass of wine, she settled down with her iPad. A cursory glance at her emails indicated she hadn't missed much and only needed to turn up for the regular department meeting the next day.

Scanning the newsfeed app didn't bring up much of interest either. She might have skipped the article altogether if the name hadn't jumped out at her: *RV Caspian*. Wreck found. Skeletal remains identified.

She opened the page to read the full article although there wasn't much more in it. A rumour was circulating, though, that there was a survivor from the wreck, but the Faroese authorities hadn't named anyone. A shiver ran through her. Lynne didn't believe in the supernatural, but the image of Charlotte Summersbridge immediately appeared in the forefront of her mind, blurring the screen in front of her.

A loud meow startled her. Babs was looking up from the floor expectantly. Lynne put the iPad aside and patted her knee. "Come on up, then, fuzzball. I guess I'm forgiven."

Babs leapt up, turned around three times, then settled on her lap. The purring started almost immediately. Slinky approached at a sedate pace, then jumped up to settle on the sofa next to her. Lynne's hands were occupied with stroking each of her furry companions.

If only the occupant of her bed could be persuaded to let her use her hands to the same effect. After the last few days in Corsica with Amanda being the most relaxed Lynn had seen her during the whole trip, Lynne started to hope she might be in with a chance. When Amanda said she couldn't face going back to her apartment right away, Lynne had been quick to offer her flat as a temporary refuge.

Her bed was only a standard double size. The one they'd shared in the honeymoon suite in Corsica had been large enough to avoid contact. She wasn't sure how she was going to cope with having Amanda's enticing body in close proximity. A few nights sleeping on the couch would be the only solution.

†

Konrad was playing a game with Ritchie, hiding the dog's favourite toy behind his back and making it squeak before throwing it across the room. Ritchie was old enough not to fall for any such tricks, but he was enjoying the attention of this new person. His immediate acceptance of the stranger was no doubt helped by the clothes Jay had found for Konrad to wear: a tracksuit Josh had outgrown. The boy was looking one hundred percent better than when she'd first seen him that morning. Hot food and a bath had improved his disposition as well. He no longer looked frightened.

Jay heard the front door close and waited at the top of the stairs. Sometimes Josh came straight up after coming home from work. Today, though, he went into his bedroom. She didn't have long to wait before hearing the downstairs toilet flush, and a few minutes later, Josh appeared, having changed his work clothes for jeans and a sweatshirt.

"Hi, Mum. What's up?"

"We have a visitor."

"Charley? Is she here?" He reached the landing and tried to look past her into the living room.

"No. She's in Norfolk. It's her son."

Jay stood aside, and Josh went in ahead of her. Konrad looked up from his position on the floor and quickly got to his feet.

"Hi. I'm Josh."

"Konrad." He held out his hand.

Jay held her breath as Josh didn't look like he was going to shake it. His next move took her and Konrad by surprise.

"Fuck that, you're my brother." Josh moved closer and gave Konrad a hug before stepping back to study his face. Turning back to look at Jay, one arm still around the startled Konrad's shoulders, he said, "Do we look alike?"

"Yes. At least, you would if you lost the fuzz on your face."

Josh stroked the stubble on his chin and grinned at her. "Maybe I'll shave it off, then."

It was a constant source of banter between them. Jay doubted he would actually take a razor to the facial hair. She knew that the growth helped him feel more secure in his identity.

"So Konrad, has the old lady offered you a beer?"

"He's only fourteen. And less of the 'old' if you want to see your next birthday."

Josh ignored her and turned to Konrad. "Would you like a beer?"

He nodded.

"Excellent. Glass of red, Mum?"

"Why not? Might as well join you in corrupting this youth."

Konrad didn't quite seem to be following the conversation, but Jay guessed he knew enough since he went with Josh into the kitchen. They were both smiling when they returned with the drinks. Ritchie dithered between wanting to sit by Josh for gracing his new friend with his presence. When they sat on the sofa, he quickly jumped up to claim the space between them.

CHAPTER THIRTEEN

I wake to see a weak trail of sunlight casting a glow across the wooden beams above. Every knot and crack familiar to me. Dressing quickly, I go outside. Watching the sun rise over the sea was a favourite part of my day. A stroll along the beach beckons, and I obey the summons. Breakfast can wait.

The walk invigorates my senses, dissipating the anxieties of the day before. Back at the cottage, I prepare the coffee machine as I had seen Mo do it. Examining the contents of the fridge, I decide on toast and marmalade. The supplies she brought yesterday include a jar of rollmop herring. My stomach churns at the thought of eating it. I suppose she thought it would be a favourite delicacy.

Breakfast over, I decide to look in the attic while I'm feeling strong. I expect layers of dust to fall on me as I pull down the ladder. But it's clean. When I poke my head into the space below the eaves and switch on the light, it all looks tidy and cared for.

The sagging armchair I recognise. One of the first pieces of furniture I bought when I moved here. A photograph album is open on the overturned crate. Possibly the same crate that held my music collection. Has Jay kept the albums? There was no sign of a record player downstairs.

I back down the steps and take a deep breath. Revisiting my past was feeling less like a good idea now I was here.

Instead, I walk across the hall and open the door to the room I resisted visiting last night. The baby's room. Jay helped decorate it on one of her flying visits between tennis tournaments. We had argued endlessly about the colour scheme. But we agreed on one thing: it wasn't going to be either pink or blue. The sea green on two walls and yellow on the other contrasted with the stonework on the side with the window. The overall effect was bright and cosy. A mobile of dancing dolphins hung above the cot.

My initial thought as I walk into the room is that Konrad would love it. I'm standing in what could be a replica of a cabin, the captain's quarters in an old sailing ship. Wood-lined walls, a built-in bunk bed with drawers underneath, an ancient-looking writing desk under the window, polished floorboards with a brightly patterned rug covering the space between the door and the bed.

It has a definite masculine feel. I walk over to the window and pick up the model of the *Golden Hind* from the ledge. Holding it up to the light, I can see the intricate detail. This was not made from a kit. I replace it gently. On closer examination, each piece of furniture in the room looks to be handcrafted. The only anomaly in this seafarer's shrine is the cowboy Stetson sitting on the top bunk.

I stumble back into the kitchen and pour another coffee. It's still warm. A strange noise penetrates the jumble of thoughts going through my mind.

The phone is lying on the table, vibrating with the sound it's making, and I see Mo's name on the screen.

"Hello."

"Morning. Did you sleep all right?"

Somehow, I don't think she's calling to enquire whether or not I had a good night's sleep.

"On and off."

"Well, before I head back to London, there's something I need to talk to you about. Is it okay for me to stop by now?"

"Yes, that's fine. I'll refresh the coffee pot."

"No need. I've had my fill here. Don't want too many pit stops on my trip back."

I take a few sips of the rapidly cooling coffee before tipping the rest down the sink. She will be here in a few minutes, so I go and sit in the conservatory to wait. This is a nice addition to the cottage. A japanese-style screen hides the exercise bike and small rack of weights. Evidence of how Jay has managed to keep in shape. I only wish I could be so disciplined. Self-consciously I pull in my slack stomach muscles.

I can't think what else Mo needs to tell me. She already talked me through the financial situation as we drove here yesterday. It seems Jay never really believed I was gone forever. She set up a trust fund in my name. And although she paid off the mortgage here, the cottage is still in our joint names. So I have a place to live and enough money to get by on without having to think of getting a job. Konrad might not be happy living out here, though. I could see he was excited at the prospect of moving to a city.

He will be getting a taste of it in Copenhagen. Last time I spoke to him, he had just been to see a film and was enthusing about another that he wanted to see. He was getting a phone too and I'm sure that will keep him happy for a while longer.

†

Jay walked through the living room quietly. But when she stopped to look at the sleeping boy, she realised a brass band wouldn't have woken him. Smiling to herself, she carried on into the kitchen. The smell of coffee and frying bacon would probably be effective in getting him up.

While she was setting the table for three, Josh appeared, followed by Ritchie.

"He's been out and done his business."

"Good."

Without being asked, Josh poured three glasses of orange juice and got the bread out for toast. Ritchie had gobbled down his own breakfast and sat by the table, watching Jay's every move as she started to fry the bacon.

"Do you want to see if sleepyhead next door is ready to get up?"

"Okay." He hesitated in the doorway. "Um, we stayed up for a bit after you went to bed."

"I know. I could hear your voices."

"Oh, sorry. We didn't keep you awake, did we?"

"No. I was reading." Not strictly true. Whatever words were on the pages of the book hadn't got past her eyes to her brain.

"Well, we both think we should go to the cottage. Konrad wants to see his mum, and I want to meet her."

"I don't know that's such a good idea right now. When I spoke to Mo yesterday, she said Charley had made it clear she wanted to be alone for a bit."

"Why wouldn't she want to see us?"

"I imagine she has a lot to process."

"Like what? We're her family."

"I've no idea what's going through her mind. But think of it this way. For twenty-three years, she has lived as someone else. And now she's having to reconcile who she was before that to who she is just remembering she is now. We've lived those twenty-three years knowing who we are, but she hasn't."

"Maybe we can help by being there for her." Josh clearly wasn't ready to give up.

"Well, let's eat first. This is almost ready."

The doorbell rang just as they'd sat down in the living room with second cups of coffee, breakfast having been consumed and dishes cleared away.

Jay ushered Konrad to the stairs leading to her bedroom, miming for him to stay quiet while Josh went down to answer the door. He came back up followed by Tess and another young woman.

"Hi. Sorry to barge in on you. Have you seen the papers this morning?"

"No."

Tess reached into her bag and pulled out her laptop. The other woman looked around, her eyes settling on Jay.

"I'm Alice, Tess's partner. I thought a phone call would have done, but she wanted to see you in person."

"Pleased to meet you."

Tess looked up. "I thought you should see this. Shit, this story is just going to run and run." She placed the laptop on the table and turned the screen towards Jay. "Some idiots have started comparing Char to Reggie Perrin. Even though that was totally fictional. All the questions: where has she been, why has she come back now, how did she survive?"

Jay looked at the heading of the news story Tess had opened for her to view. "'Dead marine biologist rises from the sea.'"

"And then there's all the stuff trending on Twitter. One tweet calling her a mermaid already has over forty thousand likes."

"Is my name mentioned?"

"No. But I'm sure it won't take someone long to make the connection with your clinic."

Jay glanced at Josh. He was hunched over his iPad.

"I need to call Mo." She picked up her phone, but before she could find Mo's name, an incoming call lit up the screen. A number she now recognised.

"Hello. And yes, I have seen the news."

Hilde's voice, normally calm, sounded agitated. "We have journalists and television crews gathering outside the embassy. The ambassador is not happy."

"No. I guess not."

"We are preparing a press statement."

Jay held her breath, fearing the worst. The Danes had agreed to let Charley go to the cottage but insisted on knowing the location.

"We will not reveal where she is, only that she wishes to be left alone at this time."

"I don't think that will satisfy them."

"It's the best we can do for now. I thought I should let you know, as I think they will target your clinic soon as well."

"Yes. I have taken some time off and have let my staff know about the situation." Ending the call, Jay realised she should have told Hilde about Konrad. But they had enough to deal with, so perhaps it was just as well she hadn't mentioned his arrival.

"The Danish embassy is under siege." Jay stood. "I'm going to call Mo." She walked into the kitchen to gain some privacy.

†

Mo sat in the car for a few minutes, gathering her thoughts. Jay's call had given her plenty to think about. How safe would Charlotte be here once the newshounds got on her trail? Someone would soon dig up an old news item, which might give away the location of the cottage. Jay was known in the village, and a few of the old-timers would remember Charlotte too. How long before one of them decided to make a name for themselves, have their ten minutes of fame?

Charlotte was looking pensive, seated in the conservatory, when Mo rounded the corner of the cottage. Jay's other bit of news would be disturbing too. She didn't know how the woman would react to hearing that her fourteen-year-old son had managed to smuggle himself into the country. Charlotte thought he was being safely minded in Copenhagen.

Mo took in a lungful of the fresh sea air, and breathed it out slowly before calling out, "Hello."

Charlotte's smile didn't quite reach her eyes, and the dark semi-circles under them showed she hadn't slept much last night.

Mo sat in a chair opposite. "There have been a few developments. The news of your survival has reached the media. Jay phoned just after I talked to you. The Danish embassy is swamped with journos camped outside."

"Oh. They won't...."

"No. Jay says they only plan to say you want to be left alone for now. But I don't think that will hold the more determined reporters off for long."

"Do you think I will be safe here?"

"For a few days, maybe. I think you would have been safer staying at the embassy."

"I needed to get out of there. I have to find myself again." A short, bitter laugh escaped her throat. "That sounds crazy, doesn't it? I'm fifty-three, not fifteen."

But why do you have to find yourself in an isolated cottage miles from the nearest police station? Mo kept this thought to herself. If Charlotte intended to stay, there was no point putting more worries into her head. On that score, she decided to keep the news of Konrad's arrival to herself. The boy was Jay's problem. Mo had already told her she should hand him over to the Danes without delay.

"Have you got enough food for now? I won't be able to come back until next weekend."

"Yes. If I run out I can go to the corner shop in the village."

"That closed down years ago. I've not walked it myself, but I understand it's a good two miles to Salthouse from here. And that's the short route across the fields."

"Oh, yes. I've done that before, many times."

Mo could see she would be wasting her time trying to convince Charlotte to leave with her. She was determined to stay at the cottage.

"If you do go out, particularly to the village here, you'll attract attention. It's not like the summer months when you could blend in with the ramblers and twitchers."

"All right. If needs be, I can survive on the tins of soup and beans in the cupboard. Oh, and there's something you can take away with you."

Charlotte went into the kitchen and returned moments later. She handed Mo the jar of rollmop herrings. "I know you meant well, but I won't eat these."

"Sorry. I thought it was a staple of your diet on the island."

"Fresh herring, yes. Not these long-dead pickled things. I never really acquired a taste for whale meat either."

"Just as well. Not something you can pick up at the shops around here. Right, well if there's nothing else you need I'll be off." She stood to leave and was surprised when Charlotte pulled her into a hug.

"Thank you for everything."

Mo inhaled the scent of the woman, recognising the tangy smell of the marine-essence shampoo Jay used. She'd asked her once why she didn't just use a regular shampoo. But even as she asked the question, she knew the answer. Simply, it reminded Jay of her lost love.

Driving down the narrow lane back to the main road, Mo shook her head. Unbelievably, against all the odds, the selkie had come back for Jay.

†

"Tess, slow down." Alice was gripping the sides of her seat with both hands. Out of the corner of her eye, Tess could see Alice's foot pressed against an imaginary brake. She eased off the gas pedal, and watched the speedometer drop to seventy-five mph. As she moved into the middle lane, two cars streaked past on the outside, probably hitting ninety.

"This is nuts. I have to be back at work tomorrow. You heard what Jay said. If anyone goes to see her first it should be her and Josh. But, unlike you, she's respecting Charley's need for privacy right now."

Tess noted Alice's use of the name *Charley*. She wavered between the childhood name she'd used, *Char*, and the more formal *Charlotte*.

"Maybe so, but I'm the one who can help her with any unwanted publicity. I've been giving this a lot of thought. We can record a carefully scripted message and post it on YouTube. That will pre-empt all the tabloids."

"And make you extremely unpopular. I don't want any part of this, Tess. We're coming up to the Stansted exit. Drop me off at the airport and I'll get a train back."

"I thought you would support me in this, at the very least."

"I can't, Tess. It's not ethical."

"Oh, so you're going to go all 'cop' on me."

"I'm just saying you should leave her alone. Give her more time. That seems to be all she's asking for. She doesn't need you rushing in going, 'Hi, I'm your daughter. Nice to meet you again. Now, if I can just ask you a few questions. Wait, I'll turn the recorder on....'"

"Shut up! That's not how I would do it. Give me some credit."

"Tess, this is the exit. Slow down or you'll miss it."

With her eyes firmly on the road ahead and no intention of slowing down, Tess didn't see Alice grab the steering wheel.

"What the fuck, Al. Let go!"

"I said, SLOW DOWN!" Alice leaned in, knocking her off balance.

A scream tore out of Tess's throat as the car veered over to the inside lane, narrowly missing a lorry. The last thing she saw was the embankment coming to meet her before the world went black.

Chapter Fourteen

I am looking at the photograph album that was on the crate in the attic. A quick look round after Mo left showed that Jay kept all my clothes, books, research notes. My previous life preserved. I didn't want to sit up there surrounded by everything. So I sit in the living room with the fire throwing out some heat and look at the pictures.

The first pages in the album show Julie as a baby, just how I remember her. I stop at a photo of me holding her with Jay beside me. Dougie took it. This is the last one taken before I left for the ill-fated trip on the *RV Caspian*.

The following pages are of Julie in various stages of growing up. As she progresses from babyhood to toddler, not much changes. At age six or seven, the little-girl look starts to disappear. A tomboy stage, I think. Nothing wrong with that. I liked climbing trees and playing in the woods as a child. But I grew out of it. Why didn't Julie? Did Jay encourage her whims? Did she think she was raising a baby dyke, in her own image?

I should have been here. I wouldn't have let my baby girl change sex.

Then I turn another page. I see a little boy beaming at the camera. It's not just the haircut or the clothes. There's something in the stance. As I turn each page, the transformation becomes clearer, more focused.

Julie, Jules, Josh. I go back to the beginning and make myself look closely at the earlier images. Barely discernible, but there's no mistaking the way the child's eyes reflect a growing sense of confidence. In the later pages, the joy of being alive shines through on the face of the young man I don't recognise.

I close the album and leave it on the table. A walk along the beach is what I need to clear my head of negative thoughts.

†

Jay sat in the visitor's chair in Mo's office, waiting for her to finish her phone call. They'd agreed to go out for a late lunch after Mo got back from Norfolk. It was now closer to teatime. They would probably end up having a drink in Mo's favourite wine bar, accompanied by a few tapas-style snacks.

The morning had been trying. Tess went off in a huff after Jay told her Charley should not be contacted by any of them. She hoped that the girlfriend, Alice, would talk some sense into her. Tess had certainly inherited Charley's short-fuse temper.

Josh offered to take Konrad out. It was a clear day for going on the London Eye. After a bit of sightseeing, he thought they might see a film. Jay took Ritchie for a long walk and was wondering what to do with herself when Mo phoned to let her know she was back and that they should meet.

†

Tess opened her eyes. There was no mistaking the hospital odours. Or the fact she was lying in a narrow bed with a thin sheet covering her. The drip attached to her arm was another clue.

"Hello." A woman in a light blue nurse's uniform was bending over her.

"Where am I?" Her voice came out in a croak.

"The hospital in Bishop's Stortford."

"How? What?"

"You were in a car accident. Your parents are here. I just came in to see if you were awake yet. Now that you are, I can remove this saline drip. Less distressing for your folks to see you hooked up."

"Alice?"

"Your passenger. Yes, she's here too. You were both lucky. It could have been a lot worse."

"Worse than what?"

"A few bruises, concussion. We were afraid you were slipping into a coma."

"And Alice?"

"A broken arm. Some severe bruising where the steering wheel hit her. Lucky not to have broken any ribs."

"It was my fault."

"She says it was hers. You can fight it out when you're both out of here." The nurse moved the equipment away from the bed and held out a glass of water with a straw.

"Make sure you drink lots of this. Just press the red button when you need more. Are you ready for your visitors?"

"Yes." Tess sipped the water and waited. She was sure she would wish she was in a coma after Donna and Cheryl found out where she'd been headed.

They came in together, holding hands. As they approached her bedside, Tess could see in their expressions a mixture of anxiety and relief. The same look they'd had when she was returned home after her failed attempt at running away. She wasn't fourteen anymore. They deserved to know the truth.

"Oh, baby. We were so worried." Cheryl picked up one of her hands and stroked it gently.

Donna took up a position on the other side of the bed, where the drip apparatus had been. She pushed the hair out of Tess's face.

Tess couldn't stop the tears.

"Sweetie, are you in pain?" Donna asked softly.

"No. I'm…oh God, I'm so sorry. Have you seen Alice? Do her parents know?"

"Yes, and yes. But they're on holiday in Spain. We said we'd call with an update after we've seen her." Cheryl smiled at her, reassuringly.

"She's going to hate me. You all are."

"You might be an idiot at times. But you're our idiot." Donna's smile chased away the anxious look that had been on her face when they came in.

"But you don't know—"

Cheryl didn't give her a chance to finish. "Time for talk later. I'll go and check on Alice and see if I can find out when you'll be released."

Tess lay back and closed her eyes. No matter what stupid stunts she'd pulled throughout her teenage years, her parents had never wavered in their love for her. She really was an idiot.

†

Windblown but happier, I walk back to the cottage with thoughts of preparing lunch. I might even have a glass of wine. After the weeks of confinement in the embassy, I'm enjoying the freedom of preparing my own meals and eating at the times of my choosing.

As I reach the patio, I hear voices. Although Mo had warned me of the impending media interest, I didn't expect anyone to arrive here so soon. I hadn't locked the door, out of habit, ingrained from living in a small community where no one did.

I step inside the conservatory and look around. There is nothing handy that could serve as a weapon. Hoping the intruders haven't come armed, I venture through to the kitchen. I am not prepared for the sight that meets my eyes.

"Konnie. What…? How…?" I can't find the words.

Konrad just grins and rushes into my arms. He is not usually so demonstrative. I hold him and look over his shoulder at the young man standing by the counter. The face I saw only days ago in the picture in Jay's office.

"Mamma, this is Josh." The words tumble out when he lets go of me. "We are brothers. And we came here in a car."

It takes me a moment to process the fact my son is speaking to me in English.

"Josh" is looking decidedly nervous. I wonder if Jay has mentioned how I reacted to the news of my baby girl's change. At first glance, there's no femininity on display. A

Deuce

closer look, even with the suggestion of a beard, gives her away. But then, I'm looking for it. I suppose she passes well enough to people who don't know her past. Prepared as I am by seeing the progressive stages of her development in the photo album, it is still a shock to see the real-life version.

We stare at each other until Konrad breaks the silence. He asks me what is wrong in his native tongue, Faroese. Nothing, I tell him, also in the language of the islands.

"Does Jay know you're here?"

This daughter, not my daughter, shakes her head.

"Well, I suggest you call her. I need to speak with Konrad. We'll go into the living room." I tell my son to follow me.

†

Jay swirled the wine around in her glass before taking a sip. She wasn't a connoisseur by any means, but it was the expected procedure in this restaurant. Taking a moment to savour the taste, she swallowed and nodded to the waiter to pour. Mo took a sip from her own glass after the waiter had finished his task, leaving the bottle and the cork on the table.

"Not bad. For a moment there I thought you were going to spit it out."

"No point in wasting it, even if I didn't like it." Jay looked across the table at her. "So, what did you two talk about on the way there?"

"She didn't say much. Spent most of the time looking out the window."

"I suppose it would bring back more memories."

"When we spoke this morning, she did ask about Dougie. Whether he knew. I told her he did but wouldn't be back in the country for a while." Mo unfolded her napkin and put it on her lap. "I gathered she's not finding it easy to think of Josh as male."

"Obviously I'm to blame for letting him transition. As if it was my decision to make."

"I'm sure she'll work it out once she meets him. I think your more immediate problem is Konrad."

"Josh will take care of him."

"For today, yes. But you really should take him to the embassy. You've got an in there, haven't you, with this Hilde?"

"It's complicated, though. I mean, what's his status? Does he automatically qualify for British nationality?"

"I don't know. You will have to let the authorities sort that out."

The waiter stopped by their table to ask if they were ready to order. Without consulting the menu, Mo rattled off the names of four dishes.

Jay sat back in her chair and drank some more wine. She hoped to be able to enjoy the food without thinking about all the complications surrounding Charley's re-entry into their lives. Her phone rang. Mo shot her a disapproving look as she took it out of her pocket.

"It's Josh. I better answer." Taking a quick look around to check that no one was seated nearby, she accepted the call.

"She hates me." Josh's voice was full of anguish.

Jay didn't think he was dating anyone. If he was having girlfriend trouble it wasn't something she was going to discuss with him in the restaurant. "Who does?"

"Charley. She could hardly bear to look at me."

A chill ran down Jay's spine. "Where are you?"

"At the cottage."

"You went there? After what we talked about this morning?"

"I know. But Konrad was desperate to see his mum. I thought it was a good idea."

And you knew if you asked me first I would have said no. Jay didn't need to voice the thought. Her silence would radiate her disapproval clearly enough.

"I don't want you driving back tonight, Josh." Jay sighed. "Maybe she'll talk to you when she's had time to calm down. Just Konrad turning up would have been a shock for her."

"But...I don't understand...the way she looked at me...."

"She remembers you as a baby girl."

"Oh."

"I'll come up tomorrow." Jay put her phone down and answered Mo's enquiring look. "Josh took Konrad to the cottage. And he's upset because Charley isn't ready to accept him. It's my fault. I should have told him how she'd reacted when I gave her the news about his transition. I thought she would have more time to think about it while at the cottage on her own. But she's not on her own now. Shit, what a mess."

The waiter brought a basket of bread and two of the dishes Mo had ordered.

"I don't think I can eat anything." Jay pushed back her chair.

"Stay." Mo poked the basket across the table towards her. "There's nothing you can do about it today. And don't even think of setting off now."

"I haven't drunk much."

"No, but there's no point arriving late at night. By the time you get back to your place, just getting out of London will take forever. I'm sure Josh can cope."

Jay picked up a breadstick and broke off the end. "I suppose you're right."

"I know I am. Now, are you going to help me eat some of this delicious-looking food? You need to eat something to soak up the wine. Otherwise, you'll still be over the limit for driving in the morning."

"Okay, okay, you win." Jay moved her chair back to close the gap and speared a prawn with her fork.

By the time they left the restaurant, she had come round to Mo's way of thinking, but she knew it would be an early start in the morning. She planned to arrive at the cottage before the inhabitants got up for breakfast.

Deuce

CHAPTER FIFTEEN

I lie awake listening to the cries of seagulls following a fishing boat. I could be back on Suðuroy. It's too early to get up. My internal clock tells me it's about four thirty or five. I don't know what to do about Konrad. I should phone Hilde. The people who were looking after him in Copenhagen will soon realise the boy is not where they thought. I can't believe they let him go to a so-called friend's house. He doesn't know anyone in Denmark. I have to admire his resourcefulness and determination, if not his methodology.

"Josh" avoided me last night. I know I didn't react well to our first meeting. I'd studied the photos during the day, so it shouldn't have been a big shock to meet in person. But it made it real. A reality I still cannot fathom, let alone accept.

I can't lie in bed any longer. After a quick trip to the bathroom, hoping the toilet flushing doesn't wake them, I go into the kitchen, put the coffee pot on, and survey the supplies in the fridge and the cupboards. We will need more food soon.

I take a mug of coffee into the living room. The fire has been re-laid with fresh logs. I know I didn't do that, but I'm grateful. One well-placed match and it isn't long before the flames start to lick around the bottom of the pile.

Opening the notebook I'd brought down from the attic, I read through the handwritten notes with a growing sense of wonder. My words, setting out the premise for my PhD thesis. Did I ever finish it? Just seeing the acronym *PDV* brings back a flood of memories. I don't need to read the conclusions of my academic writings to know there was no happy ending. Despite all the research, samples taken and examined, the cause of the virus eluded all our efforts. I know without reading it that my final observations projected the view that until we knew how to treat it, another outbreak would occur with possibly even more devastating effects on the seal population.

My coffee has gone cold, but the fire is finally giving off a good amount of heat. I feel cocooned, content. Being here always gave me that feeling. Except when Jay was around. Then I was emotionally charged up. We were either making love or arguing. Or both at the same time.

My life, it seems, has been divided into halves. The first half bursting with passion, ideas, love. The second, a half-life of mind-numbing routine, an existence rather than a life.

Konrad was the only bright spot that gave me the reason to go on living. He bursts into the room now, an enthusiastic bundle of energy. I put the book down and smile up at him.

"Sleep well?"

"Yes. Josh's room is amazing. He made all the furniture himself."

Deuce

We speak in the language he has grown up with. In the kitchen I start preparing breakfast while he chatters on, telling me about the model ship Josh built when he was twelve. Did I know there's a seal sanctuary not far away? Josh said they could go there.

"Where is Josh?" The name doesn't sit easily on my tongue.

"He went down to the beach. Said he needed some thinking time."

Avoiding me again, I guess. Konrad's hero worship is touching. Will I destroy it by telling him Josh isn't a real man?

He happily hoovers up the scrambled eggs and toast. I stick with toast and marmalade. He has to know about Josh. It will come out sooner or later.

"There's something you should know," I start off hesitantly.

He looks up from his plate.

"Josh was born a girl."

"Yeah, I know. He told me."

"That doesn't bother you?"

"Why should it?"

I stare at him, open-mouthed. He will never have met anyone who has changed sex. How has he accepted this so easily?

Konrad is giving me a strange look now.

"He explained it to me. That he was unhappy as a child. He always felt wrong. The change made him happy. He says it's like having a life, not just an existence."

I'm astounded. I don't know how to react, my own thoughts on living a half-life echoed back to me.

"Josh has these cool tattoos. Jay has them too. They had a new one done together only a few weeks ago. A leaping dolphin. He says he's going to have a half-sleeve on that arm one day. The other arm is mostly covered with a seal's head near the shoulder, and a sailing ship in the background. Can I have a tattoo?"

I shake my head. Not in answer to Konrad's question. It's all too much. Mo mentioned they held vigils on the beach every year after I was gone. Were these tattoos symbolic of their shared grief as well? No wonder this changed child of mine is likely bewildered by my lack of response towards her…him.

"He says it doesn't really hurt much. Sometimes afterwards it itches for a few days. But there's a cream you can put on."

Konrad is still talking about tattoos. I get up and pour more coffee for both of us. Then I hear it, the sound of a car coming up the lane.

†

The drive back was uncomfortable. Alice pressed herself against the door, as far away as she could get from Tess in the back seat. She had been perfectly civil to Donna and Cheryl when they were released from the hospital, but hadn't said a word to her girlfriend. *Ex-girlfriend is a possibility now.* Tess closed her eyes and tried to block out the negative thoughts crowding into her mind.

Their car was a write-off. They had only been subjected to a brief interview by the police. Since neither of them had been drinking, it was considered an unfortunate accident. No other vehicles were involved. Another motorist had phoned it

Deuce

in, having seen the car's impact with the embankment. They were concerned it was going to burst into flames.

So far her parents had been all sympathy. The hard questions would come later. Sooner than she would have liked, they arrived at the flat. Amazingly there was a parking space available on the street opposite their front door. Tess caught Cheryl's glance in the rearview mirror as she turned off the ignition. Although they'd discussed it before leaving the hospital, she wasn't looking forward to what would happen next.

"Alice, will you be okay at home on your own?"

"Yes. My sister's coming round. And my parents will be back tomorrow." Alice fumbled the door open with her good hand. Her other arm was in a sling.

"Good. We'll just pick up a few of Tess's things, and then we'll be out of your hair."

Cheryl followed Tess into the bedroom. It was as they'd left it two days ago. Letting out a big sigh, Tess opened her underwear drawer. Suddenly overwhelmed by the thought of having to pack anything, she sat on the bed.

"Do you think she'll ever forgive me?"

"Maybe. Maybe not." Cheryl sat next to her. "I know it's hard. But you need to give her some space to think things through."

"It wasn't all my fault. She grabbed the wheel."

"It's not a good idea to be apportioning blame at the moment. We're just thankful you're both alive and relatively unharmed."

"But the car...."

"Is scrap metal. If your insurance doesn't cover it you'll be relying on public transport for a while."

Tess looked around the room she had shared with Alice for the last four years. Her head slumped forward and Cheryl's arm snaked around her shoulders.

"I can live without a car. I don't think I can live without Al." She choked on the last word, the sobs starting to come thick and fast.

Cheryl held her until Tess stopped shaking, then handed her a tissue from her pocket. "Come on. You don't need to take much with you for now. Then you can come back in a few days to talk to Alice. But now is not the time, for either of you."

Tess knew she was right. There were so many things to sort out. She would welcome the support of her parents in dealing with the insurance company and replacing the essential items that hadn't survived the crash, like her laptop. At least her phone was okay. Alice's hadn't made it, though. Something else Al would hate her for, the loss of the iPhone she'd upgraded for the latest model only the week before.

With Cheryl's help, Tess managed to pack what she needed from the bedroom and the bathroom. She wanted to say goodbye to Alice, but Cheryl guided her out the front door before she could protest.

†

The drive to the cottage had never seemed so long. Jay envied Ritchie sleeping on his blanket on the front seat, unaware of the passing of time. And like an astronaut in suspended animation travelling to a distant star, he would wake to find himself in a different place, untroubled by the mechanics of getting there.

Ritchie sat up as soon as they turned up the lane, paws on the dashboard, tail wagging frantically. She wished she could feel the same enthusiasm. After the hours of imagined conversations through the night and during the drive, she wasn't looking forward to confronting an angry Charley and an upset Josh. Jay parked the Land Rover next to Josh's car.

Josh was walking up from the beach as she rounded the corner of the cottage. Ritchie bounded ahead to greet him. Jay approached more slowly, giving herself time to gauge his emotional state.

†

Amanda felt she had a turned a corner in the breakup with Jay. She was sleeping through the night, and Lynne's presence had a lot to do with that. At some point soon she would have to face going back to her apartment. But she wasn't sure she was quite ready for that yet.

One of the cats wound its way through her legs as she came out of the bathroom. Slinky, she thought it was called. Lynne had been up for a while. Amanda smelt the coffee and heard the light tapping of fingers on a keyboard. Not wanting to disturb the professor at work, she moved quietly through to the kitchen. Lynne called out to her as she reached into the cupboard for a mug.

She prepared her drink and then walked back to the living room. Lynne looked up from her laptop.

"You might want to sit down."

"What is it? Bad news?" Amanda took the chair that wasn't occupied by the other cat.

"Good news really, for someone whose name we aren't mentioning."

"You mean Jay."

"Yes." Lynne rubbed her face. "It's the weirdest thing. Quite unbelievable, in fact."

"What is?"

"Charlotte Summersbridge is alive and well."

"But…she can't be. She died, didn't she? A long time ago."

"Twenty-three years ago. Claims she lost her memory. Well, she hasn't actually said that. It's in the press statement put out by the Danish embassy. All the journos think she's holed up there and are parked outside waiting for her to come out and talk to them."

"Why the Danish embassy?"

"Well, the Ecuadorians weren't keen to have another long-term guest." Lynne grinned. "Sorry, couldn't resist. No, it's because she was living on the Faroe Islands. They don't have their own embassy, just rent space from the Danes, I guess."

Amanda sipped her coffee while she digested this information.

"Good thing we didn't get married, then." Amanda twisted a strand of loose hair away from her face. "I would still like to wear that dress, though."

Slinky had made his way onto Lynne's lap. She was looking down at him and stroking his head when she said softly, "And I would like to see you wearing it."

"It's a special-occasion sort of dress, though, not something I could…oh." Amanda put her coffee mug down and moved to sit next to Lynne on the sofa. "Do you mean…?"

Lynne was still looking at the cat, but she moved her free hand to grasp Amanda's. "I know you may not feel the same way about me, and it's probably too soon after Jay, but I would like very much to see you in that dress, walking down the aisle…."

"You want to marry me?"

Lynne glanced at her, tears falling down her face. "Yes. Not the most romantic proposal ever and I understand if you turn me down because I know you don't love me the way you loved Jay...."

Amanda put a stop to Lynne's rambling words by placing her arm around her shoulders and pulling her close.

"Perhaps we should see how I feel after this."

Slinky jumped off Lynne's lap with a startled meow as Amanda leaned in for a kiss.

†

I see them together; the dog's tail wagging between the two as they hug. My heart is pulling me towards them, while my head rebels. This is my family. I want to be part of it, but I feel distant, separated. The years of my absence have been hard on them. Jay, particularly. I think of the times I pleaded with her to give up playing tennis so we would have more time together.

She did give up because of me. I "died" and Jay raised our child without me. What right do I have to judge how she did it?

I remember the letter I wrote to her that I didn't send. It comes back to me almost word for word, a testament to my immaturity. I started writing one evening, after emptying most of a bottle of wine. No excuse, I know. I wanted to explain why I wouldn't be able to see her play in her next tournament, an important one for her, the French Open. Not so far to travel. But I was preparing for a two-week expedition at sea, taking deep-water samples, followed by the task of examining them. I told Jay I loved her, that I didn't want to lose her, but I felt our lifestyles were driving us further apart. I even laid the blame on my Celtic heritage, a tendency to accept the dark side, to recognise that my fate was to be unhappy. My bid for happiness was headed for disaster as inevitably as the deadly virus affecting the doomed seals.

Konrad comes up behind me and then pushes past. "Hi, Jay. Ritchie."

The dog hears his voice and runs to greet him. He had told me about the dog and how much he loved playing with him at Jay's house in London. Something else he now wants, along with a tattoo.

Jay's eyes meet mine as she lets go of Josh. I've seen that look before. Sad but determined. Seated next to the umpire's chair, wiping away the sweat from her face, knowing she needed to win the next game to stay in the match. I remember watching her play one particularly hard-won game, when the final set point was decided after a gruelling back-and-forth with her opponent. Each would gain the "advantage" point, only to lose it again, going back to "deuce". After that, whenever we argued, she would call out, "Deuce," to indicate we were level. No advantage gained either way. We could take a breather and start again.

"You've had a long drive," I say, stating the obvious. "I'll put the coffee on."

"I wouldn't mind some breakfast. I've brought more supplies, knowing how much these two can put away." Jay looks at Josh. "There's a bag in the Landie."

He nods and walks around to the drive without acknowledging my presence.

†

Deuce

Amanda lay in Lynne's arms, contentment spreading through her body. She wondered why it felt so different to being with Jay. Apart from the fact they had never spent a Sunday morning in bed together. When had Jay ever stayed longer than she needed to? Always rushing off somewhere, always making excuses for why she couldn't stay. The real question was why Amanda thought this would change once they were married.

Lynne made her feel wanted, loved, cherished. After only one night. Lynne's passion had been a surprise, a complete change from her calm-professor persona. An unfamiliar feeling of tenderness washed over her as she looked at her new lover's face, softened by sleep and the early morning light.

A plaintive meow from the other side of the bedroom door brought a groan from Lynne. Her eyes flickered open.

"They want feeding."

"Mm. So do I." Amanda placed a hand on Lynne's belly.

"We won't get any peace until they're fed. I won't be long."

Amanda enjoyed the view as Lynne rose from the bed and snagged her dressing gown from the back of the door. Her body glowed, and Amanda sighed when the flimsy garment covered it up.

She was dozing and looked up, sleepy-eyed, when Lynne returned bearing a tray. The enticing smells of coffee and toast roused her to struggle to a sitting position.

"I would ask you to marry me if you hadn't already popped the question."

"I can't guarantee breakfast in bed every day."

"April or May?" Amanda smiled at Lynne, wondering if she would remember the conversation they'd had in the middle of the night between bouts of exploring each other's bodies. Lynne's prompt answer didn't disappoint.

"April, I think. I can manage two weeks away during the Easter break."

"And you really do want to go to Hawaii for our honeymoon?"

"Absolutely." Lynne settled back into the bed and handed over a mug of coffee.

Prepared exactly to her tastes. Something else Jay had never mastered. Amanda didn't even mind when the two cats joined them, insinuating themselves between the two women. Slinky sniffed her toast before shuffling into a comfortable position by her side.

Lynne's eyes met hers, radiating the same level of happiness Amanda was certain showed on her own face.

Amanda raised her mug. "To us."

Lynne's smile widened as they clinked their mugs together. "I put a bottle of champagne in the fridge. I thought we could toast our engagement properly later."

Later sounded good to Amanda. Invigorated by the coffee, she was looking forward to a few more hours of discovering how much pleasure they could give each other.

Deuce

CHAPTER SIXTEEN

Jay let Josh take over the cooking. Although Konrad had already eaten, he was happy to consume two sausages and three rashers of bacon. Charley had accepted another cup of coffee and taken it to the conservatory.

Once they had eaten and cleared up, Josh said he and Konrad were going to visit the seal sanctuary. Jay was happy with this plan, which cleared the way for her to talk to Charley on her own.

Charley agreed to a walk down to the beach, and Ritchie showed his delight by running ahead of them on the path.

"So you still haven't talked to Josh." There was no point dodging the issue. Jay wasn't sure why it was an issue for Charley, though. The Faroe Islands weren't cut off from the rest of the world. They had Internet access, satellite television, movies. Maybe the people in the small fishing village she'd lived in were on the far-right spectrum of conservatism. But Charley was a scientist, a biologist. Her specialist subject was marine mammals, but she should be able to apply a scientist's logic to aspects of the human condition.

"No, I haven't."

They'd reached the end of the path and walked side by side through the sand dunes to the open expanse of beach. The tide was out, leaving the gleaming strand stretching out to meet the waves in the distance.

"I've seen the photos, though. Of her growing up." Charley turned to face Jay. "She was a beautiful girl. I just don't understand why she wanted to change."

"It's hard to explain if you haven't experienced it first-hand. I know that. And it took me a while to accept that although I was losing a daughter, I was gaining a son. Josh went through a phase of cutting himself. At first, when I saw the cuts, I just thought he was accident-prone. Then I found the razors in his room. He was only ten." Jay took a deep breath of the sea air. It always had a calming effect.

"When I finally confronted him about it, he broke down. Told me he hated his body. He wanted to be a boy. He didn't believe in God because his nightly prayers hadn't been answered. I was at a loss on how to help. But help did arrive from an unexpected source. A new client at the clinic, a trans woman. After her second treatment, I broached the subject with her. She was able to put me on to a psychologist who specialised in what they called gender dysphoria in those days."

Charley had stopped walking, and Jay stood next to her, watching Ritchie running across the wet stretch of sand to bark at the incoming waves.

Deuce

"The psychologist talked to Josh, and after a few sessions told me that this was a real problem which could only be solved by gender reassignment. Obviously I had my doubts. I needed some sessions myself to be clear on what was involved. Yes, it was distressing. I can't deny that. But at the same time, I couldn't let it go and watch Josh destroy himself. If you could have seen the change in him after being allowed to enrol at school as a boy…it was worth it. I couldn't deny him the chance for a happier life. If this is what it took, then I was willing to go with it."

"Is he happy now?"

"Yes. Each change in his body has delighted him. He was an A-star student at school, went on to study architecture at university, and now has a good job. I'm very proud of him."

Charley turned to face her, and Jay was shocked to see the tears falling rapidly. Jay wanted to pull her into a comforting hug, but she didn't know if Charley would welcome her touch. The yawning chasm of twenty-three lost years seemed like an unbridgeable gap.

Jay gestured at the distant waves. "I told Josh stories of the selkie when he was young. We would walk along here in the hopes of finding a discarded sealskin. Searching for any sign that our seal woman would return to us. How strange to think you were on one of the Faroe Islands all that time. Even though the ending of their seal-woman story is grimmer than any Grimm's fairy tale, he would often ask me to tell it again."

"Hardly a fitting bedtime story for a child." Charley had sniffed back her tears and was staring out across the sand as well.

"You've seen his bedroom. He was fascinated by anything to do with ships. Yet he never showed any interest in actually getting into a boat. Not surprising, I guess, as he knew from an early age that his mother perished at sea."

Charley turned to face her. "You kept me alive in your memories. I didn't expect that. Thank you."

Jay swallowed back the desire to hug her once more. She just smiled and suggested they make their way back to the cottage.

†

Being in her old bedroom was no comfort. Tess wanted to talk to Alice. She knew that Cheryl was right, though, and she would have to be patient. Alice wasn't the only one she needed to talk to. Donna and Cheryl were waiting for her to tell them what happened. They could probably guess from the fact the car was on the M11 heading away from London. She was going to have to own up to the consequences of her actions, her obsession. As the nurse at the hospital had said, "It could have been worse."

It could have been so much worse. One or both of them could be dead. And Alice had been right to try to stop her from reaching the Norfolk coast. What had she hoped to achieve?

"Dinner's ready, Tess." Donna's voice reached her from the bottom of the stairs.

"Okay." Tess glanced around the room again. If she was staying for longer than two nights, the Beyoncé and Spice Girls posters would have to go. She took a deep breath and walked downstairs. With any luck, her parents would wait until after they'd eaten to start the interrogation.

Guilt kicked in big time when she sat at the table and saw that Donna had prepared her favourite meal. Vegetable lasagna with a caesar salad. Her mouth watered at the aroma from the garlic bread as Cheryl brought it into the dining room.

Conversation was stilted while they ate, none of them wanting to spoil the taste of the food. The weather was a safe topic, rain and strong winds predicted for the week ahead, which would play havoc with the state of the golf course. If they weren't playing though, they would be able to watch the Tottenham versus Manchester City game on TV. Not that they supported either football team, but would like the London one to win.

After she helped Cheryl wash up, they joined Donna in the living room with refilled glasses of red wine. Tess sat in the armchair while her parents sat side by side on the sofa facing her. They were sitting close together, and Cheryl took Donna's hand before starting to speak.

"We understand your desire to meet your birth mother. We really do. But it's hard for us not to feel rejected in some way. Like we've done something wrong."

Tess squirmed in her seat. "That's not…you haven't…."

"We've always thought of you as our own. You were only three days old when we brought you home. Although neither of us actually gave birth, you were our baby. Very much wanted and loved."

"I know. I…."

"Char…Charlotte was very focused on her work. She was intent on pursuing her academic career. The few times she came to see us when you were young were mainly to talk to me about something new she'd discovered."

"It's true." Donna took over. "She didn't come round to see you. That may sound unreal. If you were in the room with us, not in bed, she would spend a few minutes speaking to you, and she did always bring a present. But then she would start talking to Cheryl about some aspect of her research which was my cue to take you away."

Tess felt tears building.

"We're not saying this to upset you, darling. It's just that we don't want you to have a false expectation of how this resurrected Charlotte might react to meeting you." Cheryl took a sip of her wine.

"But she must have wanted children. She had another child, Josh. I've met him."

"That would have been years later. She had finished her PhD thesis and was probably planning to settle down with Jay Reid with her academic future assured."

Cheryl moved over and perched on the arm of the chair, placing an arm around Tess's shoulders. Tess couldn't stop the tears now falling freely.

"We're here for you, sweetie. And we always will be."

If anything, those words only made her feel worse.

†

I know this music. I remember the names of the albums I played over and over, *Watermark* and *Shepherd Moons*.

"I didn't think you liked Enya."

Jay is stoking up the fire. I am chilled after the walk on the beach and will appreciate the warmth. The dog has already settled in his basket near the hearth.

"It's mood music and I want you to be relaxed," she says.

"Why?"

"You look like you're in pain."

"Just a few aches, mainly my shoulders. It comes and goes. A legacy, I guess, of the storm that sank the *Caspian*."

"Perhaps I can help with some massage."

"I don't know."

Deuce

Jay moves quickly, placing the sofa cushions in a line on the floor in front of the fireplace.
"Lie down on these, on your back."
"Do I need to take my clothes off?"
"No."
I hesitate, then lower myself onto the cushions. Jay kneels behind me.
"Shouldn't I lie on my front?"
"Maybe later. I just need to get a sense of what's happening first."
"Do I close my eyes?"
"It's up to you. Whatever helps you feel relaxed. Eyes closed or open. Talking or not talking."
Her fingertips gently touch the back of my head. This is the first physical contact with Jay since I came back. Am I ready for this? I'm not sure, but she hasn't asked me to undress. I'm sure a shoulder massage would involve lying face down with nothing on my torso, pressure applied while rubbing in aromatic oils. Jay isn't applying any pressure at all.
A song I know well starts playing, "Orinoco Flow". I hum along, then stop.
"It's okay. Hum or sing."
"Is this what you do at the clinic?"
"Sometimes. Depends on the client's needs."
"What are you actually doing? I can't feel anything."
"That's okay. I'm just checking the levels of tissue resistance in your body. If I use too much pressure, as with a traditional massage, then I won't be able to achieve the necessary visceral response."
"And in layman's terms?"
"Just lie back and go with the flow."

The sensation of warmth coming through her touch isn't unpleasant, and I drift off. When I open my eyes again, Jay is no longer behind me. She is holding my ankles. I can't believe I lost consciousness to the extent that I didn't know she'd moved.

Jay lets go of my feet and stands. I see she hasn't lost the ability to do so without using her hands. Something I haven't been able to do for a long time.

"Don't get up right away. Give it a few minutes. I'll make some tea."

The dog sniffs me before trotting out of the room after her. She's left the door open and when I hear the kettle come to a boil I roll off the cushions. I crawl over to the nearest chair and haul myself up to sit down. I move my shoulders experimentally. They feel fine without the creaking of joints that I'm used to. Could be something to this weird massage technique. I can't think how this healing skill has transferred from smashing a ball at high speed across a tennis court.

Jay comes in with two mugs of tea and hands me one.

"How do you feel?"

"Fine. Good, actually."

She puts her mug on the table and replaces the cushions on the sofa before sitting on it.

"When do you think Konnie and Josh will be back?" I don't stumble over the name now.

"Mid-afternoon, probably. I'm sure they'll take in a pub lunch after the sanctuary visit."

The mention of the sanctuary reminds me of the breakfast conversation with Konrad. "I hear you have some tattoos? Can I see them?"

Jay grins and raises her eyebrows. This look was usually the precursor to moving into the bedroom. I find I'm not unaffected now.

She removes her sweater and starts to slowly unbutton her shirt, all the time maintaining eye contact. My body is responding in a way it hasn't done for years. I lick my lips and know that she knows the effect she's having. Strange that I didn't react this way during the so-called massage session.

When she shrugs off her shirt, I'm not surprised to see that her torso is mainly covered with a sleeveless tee. She never did have any use for a bra. I raise my eyes from the erect nipples stretching the material across her chest.

Jay turns to the side, giving me an unrestricted view of the image on her left bicep, just below her shoulder. It's the face of a seal.

†

Jay watched for Charley's reaction as she took off her shirt. She hoped she hadn't imagined the flicker of desire as she undid the buttons.

"A seal. You and Josh both have these? Why?"

"We didn't want to forget you."

"But Josh never really knew me. She...he was only a baby."

"He was, is, part of you. I needed to keep your memory alive. He calls me Mum, but I wanted him to know where he came from." Jay pulled her shirt back on and buttoned it up to keep out the chill of the room. The fire was only a smouldering pile of ash.

"I joined the Zoological Society and I'm a volunteer seal-stranding watcher." Jay stood and placed another log on the fire. "It was another way of staying connected to you. That's why I kept this cottage too. Although if you want to stay here now, I guess that makes me homeless."

"You have the mews house in London, though."

"I did. But I signed it over to Josh last week."

Charley sighed. "You really have done everything for our child. Other than giving birth, I've provided nothing to Josh's life. I admit I was surprised to learn you hadn't continued your tennis career. I thought you would have given the baby up. With me out of the way, your path to fame and fortune was clear."

Twenty-five years earlier, Jay's temper would have flared up at such a comment. Now she just shook her head sadly. "You never did quite believe I was committed to sharing a family life with you. For the first year of your disappearance, I was a basket case. Looking after the baby was the only thing that kept me from walking into the sea. Dougie was a big support too."

The sound of a car stopping outside the cottage heralded the return of Josh and Konrad. She stood and walked out of the conservatory to meet them. When Charley followed, Jay hoped their talk had helped her to see Josh in a different light, clearing the way to acceptance.

Deuce

PART FOUR

Chapter Seventeen

Konrad is full to bursting with all the things they saw at the sanctuary. It sounds like it has grown tremendously from when I last went. Josh hangs back while Konnie assaults me with his news. I smile and open my arms. His hesitant steps towards me cut through my defenses. When he reaches my side, I envelop him in a hug.

"I'm sorry," I whisper. This seems inadequate. How can I make up for lost time? For not being there for the many significant moments in his life…first tentative steps across a room, learning new words, first day at school…all those firsts.

I don't know how long we stand there, embracing. His heart beats against my chest. My own hammers loudly in my ears. When we finally pull back to look at each other, Josh's tears mirror mine.

Nothing I can say will change the fact I've missed out on doing all the things a mother does for her child. When I gave birth to Tess, I knew I wasn't ready to be a parent. The second time around, carrying a baby I wanted to share with my partner, it felt right. I know I thought then that even if Jay didn't stay with me, I could bring up the child myself. I was stronger in every way. I think now that maybe I was wrong.

†

"Tess!"
She squinted through sleep-heavy eyes to see Donna perched on the edge of her bed.
"What? What time is it?"
"Eight o'clock."
Relief swept through Tess. She'd slept through the night for the first time since the accident. But the doctor at the hospital had told her parents to keep an eye on her to make sure she didn't sleep too long. Which was why Donna was sitting on her bed now.
"It's still early. Do I have to get up?" Tess knew she sounded like a petulant teen.
"No. But you might want to. Alice phoned."
Tess struggled to open her eyes fully. "She did?"
"Yes. And even though she thinks you're a self-obsessed moron—her words, not mine—she wants to talk to you."
"Oh." Tess sat up, releasing her grip on the duvet before remembering she was naked.
"Take it easy, Tiger. After we've had breakfast, I'll drive you over." Donna winked at her from the doorway. "You might want to take a shower."
Tess sniffed an armpit. Not too bad. Only when she was standing under the spray did the realisation hit that Donna

was hinting she might get lucky. Buoyed by this thought, she soaped herself rigorously. Had Alice already forgiven her?

†

The scene in the living room was everything Jay had envisaged over the years, a dream come to life. Charley was there, playing with Ritchie, looking on while Josh and Konrad played a third game of chess. The decider. Konrad had surprised Josh with his skill. Many years had passed since Jay had been able to beat Josh.

Charley's eyes met hers from across the room. She was looking more like the woman Jay remembered. The times they spent at the cottage were amongst her most treasured memories. She hoped this was what Charley was thinking of now, recalling the all-consuming nature of their relationship. Something she had taken for granted with the assumption Charley would always be there for her. Jay thought she could have it all, enjoying the high life while on tour, secure in the knowledge Charley was waiting for her back home.

During the intense hours of despair when news first came of the disappearance of the *RV Caspian*, Jay thought it was divine punishment for betraying Charley's trust. The times she gave in to momentary lusts, using someone else's body to fend off lonely nights in yet another city far from home. Charley had never challenged her about those affairs, if they could even be called that.

A ringtone intruded on the peaceful scene. Josh didn't react, and it took Jay a moment to realise it was hers. She plucked her phone out of her pocket and looked at the screen.

"I'll take this in the kitchen."

Hilde's voice came through loud and clear when she accepted the call.

"Is Charlotte there?"

"Yes."

"I need to speak with her immediately. Her son has disappeared in Copenhagen."

"Yes. Well, he's here."

"What? How can he be there?"

"He somehow managed to get here on his own." Jay wasn't sure how much she could say without getting him into trouble.

"He's entered the country illegally, you mean?" Hilde wasn't taken in.

"I suppose he has. But I'm sure you can fix it. After all, your people in Denmark managed to lose him, which could be embarrassing, a minor in their care. Perhaps he travelled on an emergency diplomatic visa in order to be reunited with his mother."

Jay held her breath, hoping she hadn't pushed it too far with this outrageous suggestion.

"I will have to discuss it with my superiors. But I suppose that could be a solution. May I speak with Charlotte now?"

"Yes, of course."

Jay couldn't hear the other side of the conversation carried out in a language she didn't understand, but Charley was smiling when she ended the call and handed the phone back.

"Is it going to be okay?"

"Yes, I think so. But they want me to go back to give an interview. I'm not sure I'm ready for that."

The phone vibrated in Jay's hand with another incoming call.

"I'm popular this evening." She accepted the call. "Hi, Mo."

†

Tess hoped Alice was alone as she entered the flat. She didn't feel up to facing a tag team if her sister was still there. Deirdre wasn't her biggest fan at the best of times.

"Hello!"

"In the kitchen."

Alice was standing by the counter, pouring coffee into two mugs. "Deirdre just left. She wanted to stay, but I told her that screaming at you wasn't going to be helpful."

"Thanks." Tess took a mug and sat at the table. A packet of her favourite biscuits was sitting unopened close to hand. It looked like a peace offering.

Alice faced her, sitting back, letting the arm in the sling rest against her stomach.

Tess took this as her cue to speak up. "I'm sorry. I know I can keep saying that but it's not going to make any difference to the fact I acted like an idiot and almost killed us both."

"I was going to say the same. I shouldn't have grabbed the wheel."

They sat looking at each other in silence until Alice said, "Are you going to open those? It's kind of hard one-handed."

Tess ripped the packet open and held it out. After they'd eaten two biscuits each and drunk most of their coffee, she felt brave enough to ask, "Can I come back?"

"Yes."

"Good. I know they liked having me there, but I think I'm cramping their style?"

"Your parents still have sex?"

Deuce

"Yeah. They even hold hands when they go for a walk."

"Weird."

Tess shoved another biscuit in her mouth. She had a feeling Alice wanted to tell her something. She finished chewing.

"What is it? Or do I have to finish all of these before you tell me?"

"I put my application in."

"Oh."

Alice reached across the table with her good arm. "I know you're not happy about it, but I really want to do this. My supervisor thinks it's the right move for me. I'll get all the training for dealing with incidents."

"That's what worries me. At the moment, you don't have to get involved. You just call a proper policeman."

"You'll like the uniform."

"I like the current one."

"Oh, come on. I just look like a traffic warden. And most of the time, walking around, that's what I feel like too."

"You look like a sexy traffic warden, though."

"You have sexy thoughts about traffic wardens? That's even weirder than your parents having sex at their age."

"And your parents don't?"

"No. They gave up after Deirdre was born."

"Understandable. Your sister's a walking advert for contraception."

Alice didn't respond to Tess's joke. Instead, she leant forward and asked, "How's your head?"

"Fine. My neck and shoulders still feel very stiff, but I haven't got whiplash and the doctor said the stiffness will wear off. Everything got jarred with the impact."

"I know. I'm feeling the same. But some mutual massage might help."

Tess homed in on Alice's body language. It was an invitation she hadn't expected. After the initial thaw, she thought they would have to wade through some piles of slush before reaching solid ground in their relationship.

"Are you taking special medication?" Tess asked.

"You think I need to be on drugs to want your hands on my body?"

The teasing tone was all Tess needed to know the offer was genuine. She stood and walked around the table. Alice met her and they hugged awkwardly.

"Undressing one-handed must be difficult."

"Yes, it is."

"I can help you with that."

"I hoped you would."

Tess took her good hand and led the way into their bedroom. After she removed the sling, Alice's pyjamas came off easily, but when Tess saw the livid bruise covering most of her left side, she broke down in tears.

"Al. I'm so, so sorry."

"Don't be. We're both alive. Hurry up and get naked."

Tess dried her tears on the front of her top as she pulled it over her head. She finished undressing herself quickly and lay down next to Alice. The sensation of skin on skin was intoxicating. Mindful of the cast, Tess enjoyed the first taste of Alice's lips before slipping her tongue in. She let her hand roam down to take hold of a breast, and the moan escaping from her lover's throat was enough to release any remaining inhibitions in her mind. Tess gave herself to the pleasurable task of making love.

Deuce

CHAPTER EIGHTEEN

I lie in bed staring at the wooden beams. Jay is sleeping on the sofa, which she assured me was comfortable enough. Dougie always sleeps there when he visits. I try to imagine them as a family unit. Dougie and Jay acting as surrogate parents to my child. But they are the only parents he has known.

Having spent the evening with him, talking and laughing, I'm seeing Josh as he wants to be seen. He carries it off well. The little girl he once was is no longer evident.

I want to stay here, feeling safe and out of the public eye. But Hilde made it clear I have to return to London. They want me to give an interview. Jay agrees. I asked if I would be able to meet the interviewer beforehand and Jay assured me Mo would find out who was available and make the arrangements. If possible, she could try to get a presenter who was "on our bus." A phrase I had forgotten. Jay had to explain what it meant.

But then Jay asked if I was still a lesbian, if Konrad was fathered in the usual way. We sat down in the kitchen and I told her the story.

The man who found me washed up on the sand like a beached seal was a fisherman. He took me to his house and brought me back to life. When he realised I had no memory of who I was or how I got there, he named me Katrin. Later I took his surname, Nielsen. He introduced me as his wife. I think the villagers thought he'd bought me. Although I didn't stand out as different. Celtic ancestry is common amongst the native islanders.

Jay asked why he didn't alert the authorities. He must have realised I didn't just wash up on the shore like a stranded seal. I have no good answer for that. My recollection of that time is vague. I couldn't even speak for several months. With little else cluttering up my mind, I absorbed the language, and when I did eventually start speaking, it was in Faroese.

Of course, once I had sufficiently recovered, he expected me to fulfil wifely duties. I didn't mind cooking and cleaning, but having sex with him was an ordeal. Luckily he did spend weeks away on deep-sea-fishing trawlers. And on one occasion, he didn't come back. There were many nights with Thorin where I wished for death, my own as well as his. I knew no life before him and couldn't envision a way to escape.

The ship's owners said he got caught up in some netting and drowned. There were rumours, though, that he was pushed. I gathered he was as popular with the crew as he was around the village. Which is why they thought I was a mail-order bride. No other woman would have him.

I had been living with him for two years by then, so the locals had accepted me as his wife. I received a sum of money as compensation for his death.

I was happy enough living on my own, relieved not to have to endure Thorin's unwelcome sexual advances. Maybe I was starting to come back to myself in those years.

Daily chores mostly consisted of cleaning and gutting the previous night's catch, digging up potatoes, or the job I most dreaded...butchering sheep and preparing strips of wind-dried mutton.

When the village council decided to open a library, I offered to manage it, which gave me a few days respite each month from the messier food-related tasks. The library was nothing fancy, just an unused farm building that was crudely converted to hold a few shelves' worth of books. They couldn't afford a computerised system, so I catalogued the books on a card index.

Our village wasn't on the regular tourist route for the island, but we did get a few summer visitors. Konrad's father was one of these. He arrived on a wet and windy day and had taken shelter in my drying shed. It was clear he couldn't carry on with his coastal walk until the winds died down, so I offered him a bed for the night. I hadn't intended that to be my own bed. But we sat up drinking and talking. In the morning, bright sunshine greeted us. We had breakfast together, then he thanked me and walked away.

What Thorin hadn't succeeded in doing in over two years, this stranger accomplished in one night. I didn't even know his full name. I'd mostly forgotten about him by the time I realised I was pregnant. When Konrad first asked about his father, I told him the truth. A passing tourist called Jim. He may have been American or Canadian. My knowledge of the English language was as rudimentary as most of the other villagers'. Jim and I had communicated mainly with a combination of mime and the few common words we shared.

Although telling Jay all this explained Konrad's conception, it didn't answer her question. During my time on the island, I was identified as Thorin's wife, Thorin's widow, Konrad's mother. Had I felt any stirrings of attraction to any of the women there? Some of them became friends. But that was all.

Lying in bed in the cottage, thinking of my reaction to Jay taking off her shirt to show me her tattoos, I wonder if I ever was truly a lesbian. The only woman I had ever been in love with was sleeping in the next room.

†

Making up the sofa bed, Jay wondered if it was as comfortable as Dougie claimed. She thought he was likely being kind. His nomadic life on the oilrigs and petroleum-producing sites around the world meant he was used to sleeping in all kinds of rough-and-ready accommodation.

The mattress was softer than she liked, but it would be fine for one night. Ritchie claimed a spot near her feet, having tramped up and down to find the perfect place. He usually slept with Josh at the mews house, but the narrow bunk bed at the cottage wasn't to his liking. If Josh rolled over in his sleep Ritchie was dumped on the floor.

The day had turned out better than she'd expected on the drive up from London. Her fears of the night before had been allayed with Charley's gradual thawing and finally an acceptance of Josh. Although Charley had opened up, telling her a bit about her life on the island, Jay knew there was more work to do if they were to regain any level of intimacy. Jay didn't think Charley was ready for that, any more than she was ready to face the press. Hilde's phone call, followed by Mo's, had burst the bubble of contentment she thought Charley had started to experience during this time at the cottage. A short evening of playing happy families couldn't protect her from the publicity storm awaiting her.

She had been through so much. Maybe Charley thought she could slip quietly back into her old life without any fuss. That might have been possible even twenty years earlier, but technology had pushed global communication far beyond what Charley had known in the mid-nineteen-nineties.

Jay sat up, disturbing Ritchie, who grumbled softly before settling back to sleep again. They should talk to Tess. What was the point of having a journalist in the family if you couldn't call on them in an hour of need?

She reached for her phone and poked the screen. Eleven forty-eight. Too late to call her now. She would text her first thing in the morning to set up a meeting when they arrived back in London.

†

Tess woke to find herself curled up against Alice, spooning an unfamiliar left side. Her hand brushed against the cast. The rigidity of the casing on the broken arm had led to some interesting positions in their lovemaking but hadn't hampered the satisfactory results. Tess inhaled her lover's scent greedily.

Recalling their conversation from the day before, she knew Al had played on her guilt with her announcement about applying to join the police force. Tess couldn't object too strenuously after what she'd put Alice through.

Tess extricated herself from the bed slowly and went into the bathroom. She hoped Alice would manage to sleep through the noise of the shower.

She was dressed and putting the finishing touches to a breakfast of french toast and bacon before Alice emerged sleepy-eyed from the bedroom. She'd managed to pull on her pyjama bottoms but the top was dangling across her shoulders.

"Could you help me with this?"

Averting her eyes from the two nipples standing to attention on Alice's chest, Tess managed the awkward manoeuvre of getting the injured arm into a sleeve. As she did up the buttons, her hands lingered over the breasts.

"I know what you're thinking. They're cold, that's all."

"I could warm them up for you."

"They'll still be there after we eat. This looks amazing."

Tess gave a mock pout and turned her attention to plating up their breakfast and pouring coffee.

"Mm. This is delicious. You can definitely stay."

"Gee, thanks. Was Deirdre's cooking not up to your demanding standards?"

"She can make toast. Her coffee's too weak. But she's a tea drinker, so she doesn't really get coffee."

Tess's phone pinged and she glanced at the screen to see who was sending the message. There were two she'd missed.

"Is that Cheryl or Donna checking up on you?"

"No, it's..." Tess put her fork down. "It's Jay Reid. She wants to know if I can meet them today at her house."

"Them. Does that mean what I think it means?"

"Yeah. Wow. I hope so."

Deuce

"Can I come with you? I'd like to meet the woman I almost got killed for."

Tess looked at her. More emotional blackmail. "Okay. But you'll have to wear something other than your PJs."

Alice looked down at herself. "I don't know. I think they're quite fetching."

"In your dreams. When you were six."

"Oh, come on. Who doesn't like Paddington Bear?"

Tess rolled her eyes and picked up her phone. She answered, *Yes, what time?* Seconds later, the return message read, *1pm*. It was going on eleven now, so there was no rush. She wondered what had brought about the sudden request. Maybe she was going to get her exclusive interview after all.

"Right, I'll wash up. You go and see what you can find to wear. A tracksuit would be okay."

Feeling energised for the first time since the accident, Tess wanted to get on her laptop and revise her list of questions. Then she remembered the laptop had been a casualty. Her files should be saved in the cloud, though. She left the dishes in the sink and picked up her phone.

Chapter Nineteen

I try not to disturb Jay as I tiptoe through the living room to the kitchen. She doesn't wake when Ritchie jumps off the sofa to follow me. The pervasive aroma of coffee will soon draw out all the sleeping inhabitants. My mastery of the coffee machine in just a few days gives me a feeling of accomplishment. As I look out of the window at the lightening sky, I think it is these small things that can make life seem worthwhile.

I roll my shoulders. They are clear of the aches and creaks I'm used to. Jay's strange massage that didn't feel like she manipulated anything has worked wonders. I must ask her to explain it to me in more depth.

Ritchie nudges my leg as I open the fridge. I look down at his hope-filled little face.

"You'll have to go and wake Jay or Josh. I know where your food is kept, but I don't want to overfeed you."

If he understands the words at all, his look implies that overfeeding is not a problem. Imminent starvation is likely, though, if I don't fill his bowl soon.

"Don't you need to go to the bathroom first? I know I do."

He wags his tail enthusiastically. I let him out and go into the bathroom to see to my own needs. When I come out, Jay is in the kitchen preparing Ritchie's food. I stand in the doorway admiring the view. She's wearing only a tank top and shorts. Her body has lost none of its athletic shape in the intervening years. It also seems to be having an effect on my own body, a reflexive response signalling my desire? The doubts I harboured during the night fade into insignificance. The attraction is definitely still there.

The only doubt that remains...does she still want me?

She turns and the smile that greets me sends another jolt through my solar plexus and below.

"There's not much here for breakfast. Ritchie's all right, but the rest of us will have to share what's left of the bread. I've thawed out the half-loaf that was in the freezer. We'll have to stop at the first services en route for a top-up."

When she bends down to place Ritchie's bowl on the floor, I am treated to a tempting view of her toned backside.

What am I thinking? I'm a post-menopausal woman who has given birth to three children. I can't imagine that Jay will be remotely interested in re-engaging with my wrinkled and sagging parts.

"I'll go and get dressed."

I catch a wink when she walks past, as if she's read my mind.

We have finished all the toasted bread between us. That's when Jay mentions she has thought of contacting Tess to help with ideas for talking to the press. Josh is immediately enthused, saying Tess is dying to meet me.

I realise that since arriving at the cottage, I haven't given any thought to reuniting with the young woman I gave birth to so long ago.

They are all looking at me to judge my reaction.

"Yes, I would like that."

"Great. I'll text her now."

†

Jay was surprised when Konrad said he would like to travel back with her. She had seen him conferring with Charley but expected him to want to go with Josh.

Charley came over to the Land Rover after Konrad and Ritchie had climbed in.

"I thought it would be good to spend some time alone with Josh. Are you okay with that?"

"Of course. You don't need to ask. And I'm sure he's delighted."

"Well, if he's fed up with my company by then, we can change over when we stop for our second breakfast."

"It may be Konrad who wants to switch. This old Landie isn't the most comfortable ride."

"Yes, the novelty may wear off quickly. At the moment, he's relishing all these new experiences."

"Great. Well, we'll see you there. I'm sure you and Josh will arrive ahead of us."

A look of alarm crossed Charley's face.

"Don't worry, he's a good driver." Jay grinned. "He didn't learn from me. He had a proper instructor."

Deuce

†

I study Josh's hands as he rests them on the steering wheel. They are smoother than a man's would be, I think. In profile, he passes well enough. There is a slight bulge in his jeans.

He looks over and sees where my eyes have strayed.

"It's a pack-up."

I flush at being caught staring at his crotch. "What's that?" I ask, although I can guess.

"It's a pouch that fits in my underwear, containing fake balls and a penis. I like the feel and it gives me confidence when I'm out and about."

"So you haven't had an operation…there."

"No. I'm saving up for one, but I'm still not sure if I'll go through with it."

I find it hard to imagine voluntarily going through with any kind of surgery, particularly something that would drastically change your body. There is a question nagging at me that I want to ask. But I hesitate. Jay said he'd had counselling before receiving any treatments. The question has probably been asked and answered before. But I want to know, I want to understand.

The motorway is fairly quiet and he's driving at a steady pace. We left the Land Rover behind many miles ago and will probably arrive at the rendezvous service station well ahead of it. As I'm thinking this, Josh signals and moves across to the inside lane. We are almost there.

After he's parked the car and turned off the engine, I put a hand on his arm to stop him getting out.

"I'm sorry. I have to ask this. I understand that you were very much a tomboy in your early years. I just wonder, with Jay as a role model, why you felt the need to change sex."

"You mean, why wouldn't I be happy being a butch lesbian?"

"Exactly that."

"Unfortunately it's not that simple. I just never felt right as a girl. Being a boy was all I ever wanted, dreamed about. Obviously when I was very young I wasn't worried about it. Jay let me follow my interests. Making model ships, building things. The conflict really began when I started school. I hated being forced to wear a skirt. The playground was segregated into boys on one side, girls on the other. I didn't want to join in with the skipping-rope games. I wanted to be playing football with the boys. I couldn't relate to the things girls talked about. The teachers tried to make me participate. Nothing ever worked. I just became more and more withdrawn."

"Jay said you cut yourself."

"Yeah, I was feeling pretty desperate by then. I couldn't see any way out of what I considered the ultimate horror…becoming a woman. I'm not proud of that now. Jay was devastated when she saw what I'd been doing to myself. But I was only ten. I didn't think any adults would understand. I'm just lucky Jay did."

I stare out of the windscreen. Cars and people are coming and going. Would I have been able to understand? Would I have dismissed it as a childish notion, something he would grow out of? I hate to admit I probably would have been a bad mother in this respect. Could I have listened to the concerns of my child with an open mind? I've had scientific

Deuce

training but that may not have adequately prepared me for this kind of personal crisis.

The Land Rover pulls into a space ahead of us. I squeeze Josh's arm. "Thank you for telling me this. I'm sorry it's taking me a while to catch up."

He smiles and leans in to kiss my cheek. "You're doing fine. I'm glad we can spend this time together."

Konrad waves to us. He has Ritchie on a lead. When I get out of the car, he runs over.

"I'm taking him for a 'comfort break'."

He uses the English words Jay has told him, no doubt. She comes over and says she'll put Ritchie back in the car when he's done his business. Then they'll join us in the café.

I follow Josh, making his way confidently through the throngs of people. Two coaches have disgorged their passengers, and they are all headed the same way. Josh disappears into the gents'. I find him waiting for me when I come out of the ladies'.

"How do you...?" I'm not sure how to phrase the question.

"I go in a cubicle."

"You don't feel uncomfortable?"

"I found it scary at first. But it's okay as long as you don't make eye contact. And more places are starting to have gender neutral toilets."

I'm digesting this information when Konnie and Jay arrive. We agree to order our food and drinks before they go for their 'comfort breaks'.

†

Jay sent Tess another text since there had been no reply to her first one. Maybe she had the day off, but Jay hadn't got the impression Tess was one for lazing in bed all morning.

Konrad decided he wanted to ride in Josh's car after the services stop. But he didn't want to be parted from Ritchie.

Charley was quiet when they resumed their journey, and Jay wondered what she and Josh had talked about. During the night, she'd decided she should tell Charley about Amanda. It was fairly recent history, but Jay didn't want her to find out from someone else.

There was another hour on the motorway before they reached the outskirts of London. This seemed like as good a time as any.

"There's something you should know."

Charley turned her head. "That sounds ominous."

"I almost got married."

"Well, I didn't think you'd stayed celibate for all this time."

"It's just that…well, I'm not proud of myself. I shouldn't have let it get that far. It was only ever sex for me. I know that Amanda wanted more, but I couldn't give it. That should have been a clue. I broke it off, a week before the wedding."

"That must have been hard…for her."

"Yes. I haven't seen her since. I only know she went on holiday with her friend, the one who was going to be her bridesmaid. No point in wasting the honeymoon booking, I guess. Josh was disappointed since he wouldn't get to wear the best-man's suit we had specially made for the occasion."

"So you don't regret breaking it off?"

Jay risked a sideways glance to gauge Charley's reaction. "No. It was a big relief. Like I said, I should never have agreed to get married in the first place. Strangely enough, I've since then made friends with her father. Well, a sort of friendship. I went to see him because I thought I should speak to Amanda face-to-face, having only given her the news over the phone, and she wasn't at her apartment. Anyway, he was clearly suffering from some lower-back pain, so I offered to treat him. I doubt we'll be seeing much of each other, but he did come for two treatments."

"If you succeeded in removing his pain, as you've done with mine, I'm sure he'll be eternally grateful."

"Glad to be of service." Jay didn't tell her how hard she'd had to concentrate on the process, to block out the desire threatening to rampage through her body at the sight of Charley lying on the floor, open to her touch. Her years of training and practice kicked in once she held her hands under Charley's head.

"How long were you together? You and this Amanda."

"Six months."

"You were going to marry the woman after only six months?"

"Yeah, I know. You remember the old question of what do lesbians do on a second date? Answer…hire a U-Haul. Now they don't just move in together, they get married."

"When were you able to get married here?"

"Civil partnerships were introduced in 2005 by the Labour government. Then, surprisingly, the Tories took the next step and approved the Marriage Equality bill."

Charley was silent for a time. Jay hoped she wasn't too upset after the revelation about her engagement. The next question she asked wasn't one Jay expected.

"How long have people here been able to legally change their…gender?"

Was this what she and Josh had talked about? Jay did know the answer. Josh was only eleven then and had just started using puberty blockers. She had done as much research as she could to be able to answer his questions at the time.

"In 2005."

Jay couldn't guess what's going through Charley's mind. But she seemed to have taken the first steps to accepting Josh as her son.

†

Tess and Alice stood back to let a silver Ford Fiesta pass through the archway into the mews. It came to a stop outside the door to Jay's house. A boy Tess didn't recognise got out of the passenger side. She did know the dog that leapt out after him.

As they drew closer to the vehicle, the driver rolled the window down and called out, "Hi, Tess."

She walked over to see Josh grinning up at her. "Mum and Charley will be here soon. I'm just going to park the car. Konrad will let you in."

"Who's Konrad?"

"Long story. See you in a few." He performed a neat three-point turn and drove out of the mews.

The boy had opened the door to the house and disappeared. Tess looked at Alice and shrugged. "Better go in, then."

When they arrived in the kitchen, Konrad was filling Ritchie's water bowl. He placed it on the floor for the thirsty dog before turning to greet them.

"Hi. I am Konrad."

"I'm Tess and this is Alice."

"Josh say to make coffee. Okay?"

"Yes." Tess smiled.

Deuce

He clearly knew his way around the kitchen as he set about preparing the coffee machine and locating mugs. Tess hoped he wasn't someone Josh had picked up. If he had, it was clearly a halo effect, as this Konrad looked a lot like him. A bit on the young side for a boyfriend anyway, she thought. But then she didn't know if Josh was interested in boys or girls. She hoped he wouldn't be long.

A rumbling noise under their feet startled all three of them. Only Ritchie was unperturbed. He went to stand at the top of the stairs, tail wagging.

"Oh, the garage door. That means Jay's here already." Tess grabbed Alice's good arm to steady herself. An attack of nerves assaulted her. She was finally going to meet the woman she'd been obsessing about for all these weeks.

Jay entered first and stooped to pat Ritchie's head. She was followed into the kitchen by a woman bearing some resemblance to the photos Tess had seen. Well, she couldn't have expected her to look the same after twenty-three years. The bright red hair was a more subdued shade of auburn where it wasn't flecked with grey. A face lined with age spoke of a life lived outdoors. Her blue eyes hadn't lost any of their lustre, though. And they were homed in on her.

Tess stepped forward.

†

I am entranced. This young woman standing before me is the image I had constructed for my other daughter, Julie. Even with the hormonally induced changes, I can see the similarities between the two.

"Well, Tess. You've grown." A stupid thing to say, I know. But I feel suddenly in awe of this product of my loins.

Neither of us moves. She is no doubt processing the changes in my looks too. On closer inspection of her face, I see some evidence of recent bruising. Before I can comment, Jay speaks up.

"You look like you've been in the wars."

"Car accident."

"Oh, I'm sorry. You're both okay, though."

"Yeah. Apart from this." Alice lifts the sling away from her body.

"Have you met Konrad?"

I'm glad that Jay is taking charge as Tess and I continue to stare at each other.

"Um, sort of. Josh didn't have time to introduce us properly before going off to park his car."

Konnie comes to stand beside me. I am grateful for his sturdy presence. He whispers in my ear.

I nod and look at Jay. "He wants to know if we can offer our guests biscuits."

"Yes, of course." She goes to the cupboard to remove a tin.

"Konrad is my son," I say to the two young women. I hold out my hand to Tess. "Let's go and sit in the living room and you can tell me about yourself."

That statement breaks the trance and she steps into my arms. I am surprised to feel her shaking. Jay had painted a picture of a strong-minded, strong-willed person. Telling me, laughing, that Tess was a lot like me.

Josh comes in not long after we've all seated ourselves in the living room. He sits on the floor next to Konnie and Ritchie. The three of them have formed a close bond. Male creatures huddled together.

Deuce

There. That is the first time I have consciously acknowledged Josh as male.

Tess is sitting next to me on the sofa. Alice and Jay took the two chairs. This is my family. A rush of love threatens to overwhelm me. I pick up Tess's hand and study the clear smooth skin next to my lined and liver-spotted paw. I try to keep my voice steady as I speak.

"I truly didn't know what to expect, coming back to a life that had moved on without me for so long. In a way it doesn't feel real. I keep thinking I will wake up and find myself back on the island."

We talk some more. I ask about her parents. When she tells me that Cheryl has just celebrated her sixty-fifth birthday, I am reminded again of how much time I have missed in the lives of all these people.

†

Jay was tired from the long drive and the swirl of emotions she'd been corralling all day. And most of the night as she lay awake wondering if Charley really would come back to her.

Seeing Charley with Tess was like watching a double act. They shared the same mannerisms, using their hands to emphasise points.

Josh had sent out for pizza, phoning in the order while walking back from the parking garage. The conversations started to falter once the last slice had been consumed. Jay started to think about sleeping arrangements. Josh's room was too small for Konrad to share with him again. She decided she could bed down in the back of the Land Rover, and Konrad could have the sofa. Charley might dispute the decision to let her have Jay's bed, but it seemed the best solution.

Tess and Alice finally left after agreeing that Tess would come back to talk Charley through some interview questions. Just before they left, Mo had phoned to say the BBC had a presenter lined up. Not the one we had hoped for but a woman with a good reputation as an interviewer. Friday was the proposed date for the recording to take place, scheduled for going out after the six o'clock news the following Monday.

Jay was happy that Charley could enjoy another week out of the media glare as long as no enterprising reporter tracked her to the house. Mo informed her that some unknown person on Twitter was already setting a false trail, saying Charley had been spotted in Edinburgh. Jay suspected the Danish embassy was behind that misinformation, wanting to get rid of the journalists hanging around outside their building.

As expected, Charley protested when Jay told her of the sleeping-arrangement plans.

"No. This is your house. You can't sleep in the garage."

"You're our guest. So you can't sleep there."

"Then we'll share the bed. It's big enough for two."

Jay would have argued further, but she was exhausted and gave in more easily than she might have done earlier in the day.

Ritchie was torn between taking up his usual sleeping spot with Josh or staying with Konrad on the sofa. As Jay walked through the living room from the bathroom, she wasn't surprised to see that the boy had won out. They seemed to have formed a special bond in a short time.

Deuce

Charley was already in the bed when Jay arrived in the bedroom, snuggled under the duvet. *Is she wearing anything?* Jay had donned her usual nightwear in the bathroom: T-shirt and boxer shorts. She turned off the light and slipped under the covering, carefully avoiding contact. Her hope that she would fall asleep as soon as her head hit the pillow was shattered by the proximity of Charley's body only inches away. This arrangement might have worked in a king-size bed, but in a double, one roll to the left and she would have her face planted in Charley's chest.

Trying to get that image out of her mind, Jay stilled her breathing and lay rigidly with her arms pinned to her sides. If Charley fell asleep first, she would carry out her original plan and take the spare duvet down to the garage. Sleeping in the Landie wasn't ideal, but she had done it before.

"Are you awake?" Charley's voice pierced the darkness, as soft and sexy as she remembered.

"Yes," Jay managed to croak.

A hand snaked across the narrow gap and found hers.

"I know it's been a long time and you won't want to sleep with an old woman. If you're worried I've contracted any sexually transmitted diseases from being with Thorin and Konrad's sperm donor, I can assure you I'm clear. I was given all the medical tests known to humankind during the weeks I spent in Copenhagen recently. I am attracted to you. I know we had a life together. Is there any possibility, do you think, that we could still have that?"

Tears wetted Jay's cheeks.

Charley pulled her hand away. "I'm sorry. It's too soon, I guess. I shouldn't have asked."

"No. It's not that. I'm just…oh, God…I've never stopped loving you. Loving the memory of you. And now you're here. I can't quite believe that you're real. That you won't disappear again."

The hand reached for hers again. "I'm not going anywhere, I promise."

Letting out the breath she hadn't realised she'd been holding, Jay rolled over and reached across Charley's body. She was naked, and a warm breast met her hand.

They found each other's lips, and the kiss that followed was everything Jay had dreamt of over the intervening years. Everything and more as their tongues met and danced.

When they came up for air, Charley murmured in her ear, "Take off your shirt. I want to feel you. All of you."

No more words were needed as Jay quickly shed her shirt and shorts. She lay back down, and the contact of their naked limbs connecting overwhelmed her senses.

†

"I don't know if I'll remember what to do."

"It's like riding a bike. You never forget."

"I never rode a bike."

Jay kisses me again before removing her mouth from mine to trace a line down to my chest with her tongue. I gasp as she sucks on a nipple. Already, my lower gut is responding. I don't want Jay to stop what she's doing, but I want her to keep moving down my body. She seems to know without me having to ask. Her hand trails across my stomach and rests on the curls below before she lets her fingers drift further south. I gasp as first one finger, and then another enters my wet and welcoming vagina.

Still the supreme athlete, Jay takes her time, teasing me with her tongue. First one breast, then the other. Then a slow series of exquisite sensations as she covers the area from my sternum to my pelvis, stopping just above my pubic hair. Her fingers haven't stopped their movements, in and out, a little further in each time.

I'm on the edge and want to scream, but I'm conscious of my son sleeping in the room below. When Jay's tongue finally reaches my clit, all thoughts of disturbing anyone's sleep disappear. My moans would wake the dead as I come, an orgasm the likes of which I know I haven't experienced in the last twenty-three years.

Jay lifts her head, and although I can't see her face clearly, I know she's grinning at me. The euphoria of a champion holding the trophy above her head as she parades around the court.

She kisses me and I taste myself. Jay positions her legs on either side of mine and leans back.

"Was that okay?"

"More than okay. And you know it. Now let me see if I can remember what you like."

She falls easily onto her back when I give her a light push. If I had ever ridden a bicycle, I guess I could have got back on and ridden fifty miles without mishap. Loving Jay was never a problem. When we were together, I couldn't get enough.

Now with her lying beneath me, our legs entwined, my juices coating her thighs, I know I have forgotten nothing. Our love match continues as if it was never interrupted. The rain delay hasn't tempered our desire to win, to gain the final match point.

I stroke her face. The tears are gone. "Are you ready for the replay?"

"Stop procrastinating. It's your serve. Get on with it."

And I do.

†

Waking with the early morning light peeking through a gap in the curtains, Jay savoured the feel of Charley's body spooned against hers.

Recalling the selkie legends, she remembered the descriptions of them in their human forms as being amorous, affectionate, and affable with a preference for dancing in the moonlight. The stories were romantic in nature but always ended in heartbreak for the human partners.

Charley could never be described as "affable" but she was "amorous and affectionate" and they had danced in the moonlight on many occasions.

Jay snuggled closer, placing a hand across Charley's belly. Her seal woman had returned and her heart was mending.

Deuce

Epilogue

Only a week has passed since we were gathered in this living room after coming back from the cottage. This time we are waiting for a programme to start, the television interview I recorded for the BBC. There was no shortage of journalists wanting to do the questioning. Our first choice was away covering an important sporting event. I had insisted on a female presenter and the young woman they selected turned out to be perfectly acceptable.

Tess had drawn up a list of questions, which she rehearsed with me beforehand. I didn't have time to feel nervous once we arrived at the studio.

Hilde has joined us this evening. Although the embassy has allowed Konrad to stay with me, they haven't completely let go. They have even arranged for him to have English lessons to prepare him for attending school after Christmas. Although he's already gained an impressive grasp of the language with Josh's guidance.

Both Jay and Josh have offered to give me driving lessons. One of the many things I have to relearn.

Cheryl and Donna aren't here this evening. I did meet them earlier in the week. They seemed nervous to start with. Maybe they thought I wanted to take Tess away from them. I only really wanted to thank them for being the kind of parents the girl deserved. Eventually they relaxed and we fell into our old habit of Cheryl and I talking biology, while Tess and Donna went into the kitchen to refill the drinks and snacks.

The invitation from the university came out of the blue. They would like me to attend a graduation ceremony so I can be officially presented with my doctorate. My PhD thesis was validated in my absence and a copy even resides in the British Library.

Mo was especially enthusiastic about this development and has offered to manage my speaking engagements. She is certain I will be in great demand. I'm not sure when I will be ready to do anything like that, if ever.

There is a party atmosphere in the room as the theme music for the programme begins. I can hardly bear to watch. Josh and Tess are huddled over their devices, watching the Twitter feeds and posts on other social-media sites, so they tell me. Jay and Konnie sit either side of me on the sofa.

I hardly recognise myself on the screen. The make-up artist covered over the lines and crevasses in my face and did something magical to my hair. I look twenty years younger. My voice, I'm pleased to note, comes across well. The practice sessions with Tess paid off. I waver into the emotional realm when talking about the seals and, of course, the fatal voyage of the *RV Caspian*.

Deuce

It is hard to describe those last moments on the boat, which only return to me in disturbing flashes, usually at night. I want to talk to Dougie when he comes back from Alaska. He understands about survivor's guilt. It haunted him for many years after the Piper Alpha disaster, and perhaps still does. He lost his lover, as well as many friends and colleagues on that awful day.

I lost good friends too. Anyone who has been to sea knows how dependent you are on your crewmates. But our vessel stood no chance of surviving that storm. The most experienced sailors couldn't have prevented what happened. We thought we could outrun it; instead it pursued relentlessly and destroyed us.

You can't outrun your fate, yet somehow I did. I might wish that my memory had returned sooner, that those I loved wouldn't have suffered the pain of loss for all those missing years. But then there would be no Konrad. I can't change what happened. I can only live in this moment, thankful I have made it back, able to reconnect with those I left behind. All that might have been gone forever.

My lover is here and I grip her hand as the interview draws to a close.

Josh punches the air when the programme ends. "You have your own hashtag, Charley."

I don't mind him using Jay's nickname for me. It didn't feel right for him to call me Mum. I have no idea what he means by a "hashtag".

Tess brings her iPad over to show me. There's a whole string of what she calls "tweets" with "#IAmCharlotteSummersbridge" in the messages. I'm overwhelmed by the outpouring of positive comments from all these anonymous people.

225

"You're a star, Mamma." Konnie beams at me.

Josh gets to his feet and starts to replenish everyone's drinks.

Jay leans in. "We can go back to Seal View tomorrow."

"I would like that."

The background voices, the thundering noise of the sea in my head, all recede as I gaze into her eyes. That unwavering message of love captures my heart once again.

My love…my life…restarts here.

ABOUT THE AUTHOR

JEN SILVER

After retiring from full-time work, Jen thought she would spend her days playing golf, shooting arrows, reading, and enjoying quality time with her wife (not necessarily in that order). Instead she started writing and Affinity Rainbow Publications published her debut novel, *Starting Over*, in 2014. Jen now has nine published novels to her name, a number of short stories, and not as much time as she thought for other activities.

For the characters in Jen's stories, life definitely begins at forty, and older, as they continue to discover and enjoy their appetites for adventure and romance.

Take a look at Jen's blog: www.jenjsilver.com or contact her via:

Facebook: www.facebook.com/jenjsilver
Twitter: @jenjsilver

OTHER AFFINITY BOOKS

Calling Home by Jen Silver
Sarah Frost, director of the Frost Foundation makes her home at a writers' retreats—The Lodge on the Lake. Galen Thomas, who is taking a break from her vet's practice goes to the island to fill the post of handy person. A revelation of events from forty years earlier, threatens what they now call home. Will the lives and loves of Sarah, Berry, and Galen survive the disturbing past legacy?

After Dark by Samantha Hicks
Can a love that starts out in terror be real or last? Meredith Ashcroft disappears on her way to a client meeting. Five months later, art gallery manager Stephanie Edwards is also held and tortured by the same sadistic man. Thrown together trying to overcome their shared ordeal, they find themselves falling in love. Is it true love or just an attachment to each other born out of fear for their lives?

Deuce

The Book Witch by Annette Mori
What if someone had the power to bring characters from a book to life…should they be allowed to glimpse reality? Imara is that person, a book witch who is convinced of her superiority, especially over book magicians. Join award-winning author, Annette Mori, and the gang from Asset Management, The Organization, and the colorful women in The Book Addict to bring you this delightful, magical romance.

Reach of the Heron by Angela Koenig
After an automobile accident takes the lives of her parents and nearly her own, Arkadia O'Malley faces a painful recovery. She also seeks custody of her younger sister, Rini, and contends with Irish law. Arkadia's efforts to reunite with her sister are aided by powerful women from this reality as well as from Elsewhere. Will they find her in time to save her?

From Wind and Water by Laura Kovack
Surrounded by the Lands of Earth, Fire, Water and Wind is the Seventh Kingdom. All but Earth have rulers. A new enemy threatens all Lands and it is imperative to find the last ruler of Earth. Morgayne, ruler in Land of Water and Ventus, ruler of Land of Wind, form a tentative relationship in this quest. Will they allow or deny their feelings in this fantasy adventure?

The Book Addict by Annette Mori
This is a captivating story of Tanya, a young woman whose life is without any friends or lovers. When she meets Elle, the alluring owner of the new bookstore. Tanya is immediately infatuated with the mysterious woman. Maybe, the books won't be the only thing enchanted if Elle allows the magic of love to enter her heart.

Colors of Rage by Nanisi Barrett D'Arnuk
Dr. Kailyn DeKendran, head of the Acoustic Research Department, and her sister Jayanta, are drawn into a fray of unrest. When Kailyn disappears, family and friends band together to find her. Time is running out, and the riots are getting more violent. Will they find Kailyn before it is too late to put an end to the madness that has overtaken them?

Naomi's Soul by Renee MacKenzie
This second book in the Karst Series picks up where Kai's Heart left off. Everyone is still struggling to find the balance between reconciliation and guarding. Warrior Naomi Adams is on a routine mission for the Peace Movement when a devastating earthquake strikes her contingent. She will need to dig deep to find the strength to move past what has split up her party.

My Starlight by Loryn Stone
If only we could have met sooner...
Orly Kochav likes nerdy things including beautiful girls. When she meets Danielle Cohen, the rising attraction to her

threatens to make Orly question every choice she's about to make.

True North by Ali Spooner
Cam's story continues as the Gator Girlz business thrives under her leadership. Will self-doubt jeopardize her relationship with Luce? Will a devastating injury to Sandy end her career as a gator hunter or open a door to love? Join the St. Angelo family for a third adventure to find out more about life, loving, and family in Bayou Country.

Say You Won't Go by JM Dragon & Erin O'Reilly
Logan Perry spent part of an inheritance traveling to various states. Taryn Donovan has no self-esteem and hates the waitressing job that barely keeps her in food. Can an unexpected weekend encounter turn out to be something more fulfilling? Find out in this sexually charged romance.

Affinity
Rainbow Publications

eBooks, Print, Free eBooks

Visit our website for more publications available online.

www.affinityrainbowpublications.com

Published by Affinity Rainbow Publications
A Division of Affinity eBook Press NZ LTD
Canterbury, New Zealand

Registered Company 2517228

Printed in Great Britain
by Amazon